BELTS AND BIDIS

A STORY OF A STOLEN CHILDHOOD

RIVAAN MUNGERI

Copyright © Rivaan Mungeri
All Rights Reserved.

This book has been self-published with all reasonable efforts taken to make the material error-free by the author. No part of this book shall be used, reproduced in any manner whatsoever without written permission from the author, except in the case of brief quotations embodied in critical articles and reviews.

The Author of this book is solely responsible and liable for its content including but not limited to the views, representations, descriptions, statements, information, opinions and references ["Content"]. The Content of this book shall not constitute or be construed or deemed to reflect the opinion or expression of the Publisher or Editor. Neither the Publisher nor Editor endorse or approve the Content of this book or guarantee the reliability, accuracy or completeness of the Content published herein and do not make any representations or warranties of any kind, express or implied, including but not limited to the implied warranties of merchantability, fitness for a particular purpose. The Publisher and Editor shall not be liable whatsoever for any errors, omissions, whether such errors or omissions result from negligence, accident, or any other cause or claims for loss or damages of any kind, including without limitation, indirect or consequential loss or damage arising out of use, inability to use, or about the reliability, accuracy or sufficiency of the information contained in this book.

Made with ♥ on the Notion Press Platform
www.notionpress.com

To those who offer a hand in the darkness,

a light in the storm.

You are the lifeline of hope.

Contents

1. The Corridor Of Echoes — 1
2. Lashing — 5
3. The Longest Night — 12
4. The First Drag — 20
5. Breaking Point — 33
6. Building — 50
7. The Dilemma — 66
8. Unexpected Connections — 73
9. Tender Discoveries — 89
10. Broken Glasses — 99
11. Echoes Of Her Heartbeat — 108
12. The Descent — 116
13. Like Father Like Son! — 119
14. The Wake-Up Call — 129
15. The Long Road Back — 138
16. Rebuilding — 154

Glossary — 157

CHAPTER ONE

The Corridor of Echoes

The antiseptic smell of the hospital corridor burned Dhruv's nostrils as he paced, his heart racing. The rhythmic beeping of machines punctuated the eerie silence, each sound a reminder of life's fragility. But even as the hospital's scents pressed in, another, older smell fought for dominance. Acrid smoke, the kind that clung to cheap tobacco and even cheaper alcohol, pricked at the back of his throat. It was a smell Dhruv knew intimately, a smell that tugged at the edges of his awareness, threatening to pull him under.

He ran a trembling hand through his unkempt hair, realising he couldn't remember the last time he'd showered or changed his clothes. Time had lost all meaning in this liminal space between hope and despair.

A nurse hurried past, offering Dhruv a tight-lipped smile, her eyes filled with sympathy and exhaustion. He wanted to ask for news, but the words caught in his throat. Instead, he watched her disappear around a corner, taking with her any chance of momentary comfort.

From the delivery room, a muffled cry of pain echoed through the door, causing Dhruv's heart to leap into his throat. He took an involuntary step forward, his hand reaching out as if he could offer comfort through the walls.

But the cry faded, leaving behind only the steady beep of monitors and the low murmur of medical staff.

A door opened, and Dhruv's attention snapped back to the present. A doctor emerged from the delivery room, his face etched with concern. Time seemed to slow as he approached.

"Mr. Dhruv?" The doctor's voice was low and measured, but Dhruv could hear the underlying tension. "There's a complication. We are doing.. everything we can."

The world tilted on its axis. The fluorescent lights buzzed overhead, casting a harsh glow that made everything appear washed out and unreal. The white walls of the corridor began to blur and shift, like fog dissipating in the morning sun. The steady hum of medical equipment morphed into a distant, distorted melody that Dhruv hadn't heard in years but recognised on a primal level.

Dhruv's footsteps echoed off the polished floor, creating a syncopated rhythm that mingled with the muffled sounds from nearby rooms. As if in a trance, he stopped his pacing. The cool linoleum beneath his feet seemed to shift, to roughen. The smooth surface transformed into the grain of worn wooden planks that creaked with the slightest movement.

He squeezed his eyes shut, willing the world back into focus. When he opened them again, the sterile white walls of the hospital remained. But the air... the air held the unmistakable weight of unspoken stories and buried emotions. It was the weight of his past, threatening to suffocate the fragile hope he clung to in the present.

As if emerging from a dream, Dhruv found himself in a dimly lit room. The transition was subtle, reality bleeding away at the edges until he was fully immersed in this new, yet hauntingly familiar, space. The rough wooden planks beneath his feet creaked with each tiny movement, a stark contrast to the silent linoleum of the hospital.

A lone candle flickered on a rickety table, its flame casting long, dancing shadows across the walls. Stagnant fumes of bottom-shelf liquor and burnt tobacco formed an oppressive fog, assaulting the senses. Each breath Dhruv took felt like a struggle, the smoke seeming to cling to his lungs and coat his throat.

The room itself seemed to exude an aura of neglect and lost hope. Peeling wallpaper hung in sad, faded strips, revealing the crumbling plaster beneath. Empty bottles littered every surface, their labels a testament to nights spent trying to drown sorrows in too-bit moonshine. A sagging armchair stood in one corner, its stuffing peeking out through worn seams like tufts of grey hair – a silent witness to countless hours of solitary despair.

In the background, barely audible over the pounding of blood in his ears, Dhruv could hear the faint strains of a melancholy song. The music drifted in from somewhere beyond the room, its mournful tones intertwining with the oppressive atmosphere.

A sudden gust of wind rattled the single window, its pane grimy and cracked. Through the dirt-streaked glass, Dhruv could make out the vague outlines of buildings pressed close together, their shapes indistinct in the gathering gloom of evening. The world outside seemed as bleak and hopeless as the room itself.

As he stood between two realities, Dhruv felt vertigo wash over him. The room seemed to pulse with unspoken stories and buried emotions. Somewhere in the distance, barely audible above his ragged breathing, he thought he could hear the faint beeping of hospital monitors – a tenuous link to another world, another moment in time.

Dhruv closed his eyes, trying to make sense of the conflicting sensations assaulting him. The rough wood beneath his feet, the acrid smoke in his lungs, the distant music – all felt as real as the sterile hospital corridor had moments ago. Yet even as he stood there, he could feel the memory of cool linoleum and the sting of disinfectant lingering at the edges of his consciousness.

When he opened his eyes again, the room remained unchanged. The candle still flickered, the shadows danced, and the air hung heavy with smoke and regret. Dhruv was suspended between two worlds, two moments in time, unsure of which was real and which was memory.

In this liminal space between then and now, his fears, hopes, and regrets crashed over him like a tidal wave. And there, caught in the crossroads of memory and moment, Dhruv waited for the next turn of fate's wheel, unsure of where it would take him.

CHAPTER TWO

Lashing

Stale smoke and liquor smell choked the cramped, dimly lit room. Tattered curtains, more holes than fabric, fluttered weakly in the tepid breeze that seeped through cracks in the grimy window pane. The setting sun cast long shadows across the uneven concrete floor, transforming mundane objects into ominous silhouettes.

Dhruv's fingers, clutching the frayed edges of the mattress, tightened until his knuckles ached, a stark white against the grimy fabric. He squeezed his eyes shut, his small frame trembling as the uneven, heavy footsteps drew closer. Each thud echoed in the room's silence, a drumbeat of terror mirrored the frantic pounding in his ears. *Don't be here. Please, don't be here.* But the footsteps stopped just outside his door, and Dhruv knew it was a futile prayer.

A crash— the front door was thrown open— sliced through the heavy silence. Dhruv's eyes flew open, but the last of the sun had vanished, leaving the room draped in shadows. He didn't need light to see the hulking silhouette in the doorway, its edges blurring as if the air around it vibrated with menace. The figure emitted a powerful, suffocating scent of sweat and cheap booze, a smell so intense it seemed to have a life of its own.

Don't be here. Not today. Please. Dhruv's silent plea died in the dry rasp of his throat. His heart, a frantic drum against his ribs, pounded out a rhythm of pure terror. He squeezed his eyes shut, his small frame shrinking into the threadbare mattress, wishing, praying to disappear. *Maybe he won't see me if I'm small enough or quiet enough.*

"Boy!" The voice, a guttural growl that seemed to claw its way from deep within the man's chest, shattered Dhruv's desperate hope. He knew that voice, the way it tightened with barely contained rage, how each word was a prelude to pain.

Dhruv remained still, hoping against hope that if he didn't move or breathe, his father might forget he existed. It was a futile wish, one that had never come true in all his years.

"I know you're in here, you worthless piece of shit." Ram's words slurred together, thick with alcohol and barely contained rage. He fumbled for the light switch, cursing when his clumsy fingers failed to find it immediately.

The naked bulb flickered to life, its harsh glare revealing the squalor of their existence. Peeling paint, water stains creeping across the ceiling, a broken chair propped against the wall – each detail a testament to years of neglect and poverty. Ram's bloodshot eyes fixed on Dhruv's huddled form. "Get up," he snarled, taking an unsteady step forward. "Get up and face me like a man."

Dhruv's muscles screamed in protest as he slowly pushed himself up, his back still tender from the previous night's beating. He blinked rapidly, eyes adjusting to the sudden brightness. His father's face swam into focus – unshaven, deep lines etched by years of bitterness and alcohol abuse.

"You think you can hide from me?" Ram's hand went to his waist, fingers fumbling with his belt buckle. The metallic clink sent a shudder through Dhruv's body, a Pavlovian response honed by years of abuse. "In my own house?"

"I wasn't hiding, Baba," Dhruv whispered, his voice barely audible. He knew from experience that protesting too loudly would only fuel his father's anger, but complete silence was just as dangerous.

Ram's laugh was devoid of humour, a harsh bark that seemed to scrape against Dhruv's eardrums. "Not hiding? Then what do you call this?" He gestured wildly, nearly losing his balance. "Curled up in the dark like a dog?"

Dhruv's mind raced, searching for the right words, the magic combination that might defuse his father's volatile temper. But before he could speak, Ram's hand shot out, grabbing a fistful of Dhruv's shirt and yanking him to his feet.

The boy stumbled, the sudden movement sending a wave of dizziness. He hadn't eaten since yesterday morning, his stomach a hollow ache that he'd learned to ignore.

"Look at me when I'm talking to you!" Ram shook him roughly, alcohol-soured breath hot against Dhruv's face. "You ungrateful little bastard. After everything I've done for you..."

Dhruv forced himself to meet his father's gaze, fighting against every instinct that screamed at him to look away. Ram's eyes were bloodshot, the whites yellowed from years of drinking. Up close, Dhruv could see the network of broken capillaries spreading across his father's nose and cheeks, a roadmap of addiction etched into his skin.

"I'm sorry, Baba," Dhruv murmured, the words automatic, meaningless. He'd long since lost count of how many times he'd uttered that phrase, how many times he'd apologised for simply existing.

Ram's grip tightened, his fingernails digging into Dhruv's bony shoulder. "Sorry?" he spat. "You're always sorry. But it doesn't change anything, does it? Doesn't bring her back."

The familiar ache bloomed in Dhruv's chest at the mention of his mother. He tried, as he always did, to conjure an image of her face. But like a mirage in the desert, it remained frustratingly out of reach. All he had were fragments – the ghost of a gentle touch, the fading echo of a lullaby.

"She left because of you," Ram continued, his voice rising. The words were well-worn, a litany Dhruv had heard countless times before. "Couldn't stand the sight of you. Her own son and she couldn't bear to stay."

Dhruv bit the inside of his cheek, using the sharp sting of pain to ground himself. He tasted copper, realising too late that he'd broken the skin. The metallic flavour mixed with the sour taste of fear in his mouth.

Ram released his grip suddenly, sending Dhruv stumbling backwards. The boy's legs hit the edge of the mattress, and he fell gracelessly onto its lumpy surface. A spring dug into his lower back, but he didn't dare move to adjust his position.

"Get up," Ram growled, fumbling with his belt. The leather slid free with a soft hiss, like a snake uncoiling. "Get up and take your punishment like a man."

Dhruv's heart hammered against his ribcage, threatening to burst from his chest. His palms were slick with sweat, and he could feel tremors starting in his legs.

But he forced himself to stand, knowing that disobedience would only worsen things.

The first lash caught him across the shoulders, the crack of leather against skin echoing in the small room. Dhruv's breath hitched, but he bit back the cry that threatened to escape. Tears wouldn't help; they never did.

"This is for your own good," Ram slurred, drawing his arm back for another strike. "You need to learn respect."

The belt whistled through the air, connecting with Dhruv's back. Fire erupted along the point of impact, spreading outward in a wave of agony. Dhruv's vision blurred, black spots dancing at the edges.

"Your mother left because of you!" Another lash, this one catching the sensitive skin just above Dhruv's hip. "It's all your fault!"

Dhruv's legs trembled, threatening to give out. But he locked his knees, forcing himself to remain upright. Falling now would only prolong the punishment and fuel his father's rage further.

The blows continued to rain, each stealing more of Dhruv's breath. He retreated into his mind, desperately trying to escape the pain, the humiliation, the overwhelming sense of helplessness.

In his mind's eye, he saw a woman's silhouette, backlit by a setting sun. Her face was turned away, features lost in shadow. Was this a memory or just another fabrication of his desperate imagination? Dhruv clung to the image, using it as a lifeline to weather the storm of his father's fury.

"Useless boy," Ram panted, his arm finally dropping to his side. The belt dangled from his fingers, a serpent temporarily sated. "Just like your mother. Weak. Pathetic."

Dhruv remained standing, swaying slightly. His back was on fire, each breath sending fresh waves of pain through his body. He could feel warm wetness trickling down his spine and knew without looking that his shirt would be stained with blood.

Ram stumbled backwards, collapsing heavily onto the room's only chair. It creaked ominously under his weight, one leg slightly shorter than the others. He fumbled in his pocket, producing a battered pack of cigarettes and a lighter.

The sharp scent of sulphur filled the air as Ram struck a match, cupping his hand around the flame as he lit the bidi. He took a deep drag, the tip glowing bright orange in the dimness. Smoke curled upward, adding another layer to the room's oppressive atmosphere.

"Clean yourself up," Ram muttered, not bothering to look at his son. "And don't let me catch you lazing around again. There's work to be done."

Dhruv nodded mechanically, not trusting his voice. He shuffled toward the door, each step sending jolts of pain through his battered body. The bathroom was little more than a closet, with a cracked mirror hanging crookedly above a rust-stained sink.

He avoided his reflection as he wet a ragged towel, hissing as he gingerly dabbed at the welts on his back. The cool water provided momentary relief, but Dhruv knew from experience that the real pain would set in later once the adrenaline wore off.

As he tended to his wounds, Dhruv's mind drifted once again to the shadowy figure of his mother. He strained to remember her voice, her laugh, anything concrete to hold onto. But like always, she remained just out of reach, a ghost haunting the edges of his memory.

In the other room, he could hear his father's laboured breathing, punctuated by occasional coughs. The tobacco smoke drifted under the door, its pungent odour a constant reminder of Ram's presence.

Dhruv leaned heavily against the sink, his legs finally giving out now that he was alone. He allowed himself one shuddering breath, one moment of weakness. Then, with effort, he straightened up. There was work to be done, as there always was. And tomorrow... tomorrow would be another day of walking on eggshells, trying to predict his father's moods, and existing in the shadow of a mother he couldn't remember.

He squared his shoulders, ignoring the flash of pain the movement caused. The sun had fully set now, plunging the small apartment into darkness broken only by the harsh glare of the bare bulb. Dhruv stepped out of the bathroom, ready to face whatever the night might bring, knowing that morning would come eventually. It always did.

CHAPTER THREE

The Longest Night

The hospital air, though clean, held a metallic tang that pricked at Dhruv's nostrils, a scent forever entwined with fear. The fluorescent lights buzzed overhead, casting a sickly pallor over the already pale green walls. The colour reminded him of the lime popsicles Priya had craved throughout her pregnancy. How many midnight runs had he made to the corner store to see her eyes light up as she unwrapped that coveted treat?

Now, those same green walls seemed to mock him, their colour no longer a symbol of joy but of nausea and uncertainty. Dhruv's fingers twitched at his sides, desperate for something to hold onto, something to ground him in this moment that felt like a waking nightmare.

The clock on the wall ticked relentlessly, each second an eternity. Dhruv found his eyes drawn to it repeatedly, watching the red second hand make its endless journey. How long had he been here? Hours? Days? Time had lost all meaning since they'd rushed Priya into the delivery room, her face contorted in pain, her normally melodious voice reduced to guttural screams that still echoed in his ears.

A brief commotion down the hall caught his attention – a group of nurses rushing past, their rubber-soled shoes squeaking against the polished linoleum floor. Dhruv's heart leapt into his throat. Were they heading to Priya's room? He took a half-step forward, ready to chase after them, to demand answers, but his legs felt leaden, unwilling to cooperate.

The weight of exhaustion pressed down on him. How long had it been since he'd slept and truly slept, not just fitful dozing in uncomfortable waiting room chairs? The past week had been a blur of false alarms and anxious nights, culminating in this endless vigil outside the delivery room doors.

Dhruv sat in the sterile hospital waiting room, his mind a whirlwind of anxiety and anticipation as he awaited news of his wife Priya's pregnancy. He ran a hand through his hair, wincing at the greasy texture that clung to his fingers. The need for a shower, fresh clothes, and a proper meal gnawed at him, but the mere thought of leaving, even for a moment, sent a jolt of panic through his chest. What if something happened in his absence? What if Priya called out for him, and he wasn't there?

Unable to sit still, Dhruv found his feet carrying him aimlessly through the hospital corridors. Without a conscious decision, he suddenly found himself standing before a paan shop, its familiar array of tobacco products calling to him like a siren song. Almost in a trance, he purchased a pack of bidis, the rough paper and strong tobacco, which were a comforting weight in his hand. He could have afforded cigarettes now, their sleek packaging a symbol of his improved circumstances, but the bidis were a familiar touchstone, a link to his past self.

As Dhruv returned to the hospital, each step felt heavier than the last. The pack of bidis burned in his pocket, a physical manifestation of the guilt that began to consume him. His mind raced with memories of the promise he'd made to Priya, the solemn vow to quit smoking for the sake of their unborn child. The conflict raged within him – the craving for that familiar comfort warring against the love for his family and the future they were building together. Dhruv's thoughts spiralled, torn between desire and duty, as he resumed his anxious vigil in the waiting room.

His hand moved of its own accord, muscle memory guiding his fingers to his pocket. They brushed against the familiar shape there, and for a moment, Dhruv's entire being cried out for the comfort it promised. A bidi. Just one. Just a single moment of relief in this endless nightmare.

He could almost taste it – the harsh burn of smoke in his lungs, the heady rush of nicotine flooding his system. It would calm his nerves, quiet the screaming voice in his head that kept repeating *your fault, your fault, your fault* in an endless loop.

Dhruv's fingers closed around the small packet, and the crinkle of cellophane was loud in the quiet corridor. He began to draw it out of his pocket, already anticipating the ritual – the careful unwrapping, the match flare, and the first deep inhale.

No.

The thought hit him like a bucket of ice water. Priya's voice, clear as day, echoed in his mind. *Promise me, Dhruv. Promise me you'll quit. For me. For our baby.*

With a herculean effort, Dhruv wrenched his hand away from his pocket. The bidi remained where it was, a temptation unfulfilled. He clenched his fists at his sides, nails digging into his palms. The small sparks of pain helped to ground him, to push back against the overwhelming urge to give in.

He'd promised Priya. And even now, with everything hanging in the balance, he couldn't bear the thought of breaking that promise. What if she could smell it on him when this was all over? What if it was the first thing she noticed, overshadowing the joy of their new family?

The thought of disappointing Priya was somehow worse than the gnawing fear and uncertainty. Dhruv took a deep, shuddering breath, trying to fill the void left by the absent bidi with clean, sterile hospital air.

It wasn't enough. The corridor spun around him, the green walls blurring into a nauseating whirl. Dhruv closed his eyes tightly, pressing the heels of his hands against his eyelids until he saw bursts of colour in the darkness.

With his eyes closed, the hospital faded away. In its place, memories rose unbidden, as vivid and real as the day they'd happened. Dhruv let them wash over him, too exhausted to fight against the tide of recollection.

The first time, he saw Priya in her red and golden saree, peeking shyly at him. The way his heart had stumbled in his chest, recognising her as home.

Their first real fight, over something so trivial he couldn't even remember the cause now. The sick feeling in his stomach as he'd stormed out of their tiny apartment, the overwhelming relief when he'd returned hours later to find her waiting up for him, her eyes red-rimmed but full of forgiveness.

The day Priya had burst into the kitchen, waving a positive pregnancy test like a victory flag. The mixture of elation and terror that had flooded through him as he realised he was going to be a father.

Each memory was a lifeline to cling to in the storm of fear and uncertainty. Dhruv breathed deeply, in and out, letting the familiar scenes play out behind his closed eyelids.

Gradually, the spinning sensation subsided. Dhruv opened his eyes cautiously, relieved that the corridor had stopped its nauseating dance. The green walls were once again stationary, the clock still ticking away the seconds mercilessly.

He pushed himself away from the wall on unsteady legs, pacing the short length of the corridor. Five steps one way, turn, five steps back. It wasn't much, but it was movement, action – something to stave off the helplessness that threatened to overwhelm him.

As he walked, Dhruv found his hand straying to his pocket again. The packet of bidis seemed to burn against his thigh, a constant reminder of the comfort just out of reach. He clenched his fist, trying to focus on anything else – the squeak of his shoes on the linoleum, the distant murmur of voices, the steady hum of the fluorescent lights.

But the craving persisted, a physical ache that grew stronger each minute. Dhruv's mouth felt dry, his nerves frayed to the breaking point. Just one bidi, he thought. To take the edge off. Priya would understand, wouldn't she? Given the circumstances?

No sooner had the thought formed than guilt crashed over him like a wave. How could he even consider it? Priya was in there, fighting to bring their child into the world, and here he was, contemplating breaking a promise over a moment of weakness.

The memory of Priya's face, when he'd promised to quit, rose unbidden in his mind. The pride in her eyes, the soft kiss she'd pressed to his cheek. "I knew you could do it," she'd whispered. "Our baby is so lucky to have you as a father."

Dhruv's throat tightened. What kind of father would he be if he couldn't keep this promise? If he couldn't be strong when it mattered most?

With a growl of frustration, he yanked the packet of bidis from his pocket. For a moment, he stared at it, feeling its weight in his hand. Then, with a sudden, decisive movement, he strode to the nearest trash can and dropped the packet.

The soft thud hitting the bottom of the bin seemed to echo in the quiet corridor. Dhruv stood there for a long moment, his hand still outstretched, warring emotions playing across his face.

Relief. Regret. Pride. Fear.

He'd done it. He'd resisted. But oh, how he wanted to reach back in and retrieve that packet. His fingers twitched at his sides, and he had to physically step back from the bin to stop himself from giving in.

A soft whimper behind the delivery room doors snapped Dhruv back to reality. Priya. She needed him to be strong, to be present. Not out here, fighting his own demons.

He resumed his pacing, this time with renewed purpose. Each step was a silent promise. To Priya. To their unborn child. To himself.

I am stronger than this. I am more than my cravings. I will be the husband and father my family deserves.

Time stretched on, measured only by the ticking of the clock and the soft scuff of Dhruv's shoes on the floor. The corridor remained stubbornly empty, no doctors or nurses emerging to give him the news – good or bad.

Dhruv's mind conjured a thousand scenarios, each more terrifying than the last. What if the baby was in distress? What if Priya...

No. He couldn't let himself think like that. Priya was strong. She would get through this. They both would.

A particularly loud cry echoed from behind the delivery room doors as if in response to his thoughts. Dhruv froze mid-step, his heart pounding. Was that it? Was that the moment their lives changed forever?

He strained his ears, desperate for any sound, any sign. But the corridor fell silent once more, leaving him alone with his racing thoughts and the persistent craving that gnawed at the edges of his resolve.

Dhruv's gaze fell on the trash can again, and he felt a fresh wave of longing wash over him. It would be so easy to fish out that packet, to steal away for just a moment and find some relief from this endless, agonising wait.

But no. He'd made his choice. He'd made his promise. And Dhruv was determined to keep it, no matter how difficult it might be.

Instead, he forced himself to sit in one of the hard plastic chairs lining the wall. His leg bounced nervously, fingers drumming an erratic rhythm on the armrest. Anything to keep his hands busy, to channel the restless energy that threatened to overwhelm him.

Dhruv closed his eyes, trying to focus on his breathing. In for four counts, hold for seven, out for eight. It was a technique Priya had learned in her prenatal yoga classes, one she'd insisted on practising with him. "For when the labour gets tough," she'd said with a smile that was equal parts excitement and apprehension.

Dhruv clung to the memory of those quiet evenings as he sat in that hospital corridor. Priya's soft counting, the warmth of her hand in his, the gentle swell of her belly beneath his palm. The future they'd dreamed of, so close now he could almost touch it.

A future without bidis. Without the constant craving, the guilt, and the worry about second-hand smoke harming their child. A future where he was present, fully and completely, for every precious moment.

Dhruv opened his eyes, and his resolve strengthened. Whatever happened behind those delivery room doors, whatever challenges lay ahead, he would face them with clear lungs and a steady heart. For Priya. For their baby. For the family, they were becoming.

The clock on the wall ticked on, marking the passage of time in this endless night. But for the first time since arriving at the hospital, Dhruv felt a glimmer of hope. The craving was still there, a dull ache in the back of his mind, but it no longer consumed him.

He was ready. Ready to be the man Priya believed him to be. Ready to be a father. Ready for whatever came next.

CHAPTER FOUR

The First Drag

Dhruv huddled in the corner of the small, dimly lit room he called home, his skinny arms wrapped tightly around his knees. At just eleven years old, his young face already bore the weariness of someone far beyond his years. Each footstep landed like a hammer blow, shaking the flimsy walls of his world. His body tensed in anticipation of what might come next.

The door creaked open, and Ram, Dhruv's father, stumbled in. A pungent wave of cheap liquor wafted in ahead of him, its biting aroma filling the cramped space and announcing his arrival. Dhruv held his breath, praying to become invisible, to melt into the peeling wallpaper behind him. But as always, his prayers went unanswered.

"Boy!" Ram's voice boomed, slurred but no less terrifying for it. "Where's my dinner?"

Dhruv scrambled to his feet, his heart pounding so hard he was sure it would burst from his chest. "I... I'm sorry, Baba. I'll get it right away," he stammered, edging towards the small kitchenette.

But he wasn't fast enough. Ram's hand shot out, grabbing Dhruv's thin arm with bruising force. "Sorry? You're always sorry, you useless child. Just like your mother. Sorry, sorry, sorry!"

The first blow caught Dhruv across the cheek, snapping his head to the side. He tasted blood, but he didn't cry out. Experience had taught him that tears only fuelled his father's rage. Instead, he retreated into himself, to the quiet place in his mind where the pain couldn't reach.

Later, when Ram had finally passed out on the worn sofa, Dhruv crept out of the house. His body ached, new bruises forming atop old ones, but the physical pain was nothing compared to the hollow ache in his chest. He wandered the narrow streets of their neighbourhood with no destination in mind, just a desperate need to be anywhere but home.

The tobacco scent caught his attention, drifting from a small group of men huddled near a street lamp. Dhruv watched from the shadows as they passed around small, leaf-wrapped cylinders, laughing and talking without care. He recognised the bidis from the corner shop where he sometimes ran errands for his father.

Curiosity overcame his usual caution, and Dhruv inched closer. One of the men noticed him, a kind-faced uncle with greying hair at his temples.

"Arrey, little one," the man called out. "What are you doing out so late?"

Dhruv shrugged, not meeting the man's eyes. "Just walking, uncle."

The man studied him for a moment, taking in Dhruv's dishevelled appearance and the dark bruise blooming on his cheek. Something like understanding flickered in his eyes. Without a word, he held out his hand, offering Dhruv a bidi.

"Here, beta. Sometimes a little smoke can ease a heavy heart."

Dhruv hesitated, but only for a moment. He had seen his father smoke countless cigarettes and had been breathing in second-hand smoke for years. This couldn't be much different, could it? And if it could make him feel even as carefree as these men looked...

Dhruv's trembling fingers accepted the small, leaf-wrapped cylinder. The kind-faced uncle showed him how to light it and inhale the smoke through the mouth. He raised the bidi to his lips, his heart pounding with anticipation and fear. The match flared to life, its sulphurous scent mingling with the earthy aroma of the tobacco. Dhruv inhaled deeply, drawn to the harsh smoke like a moth to a flame.

The effect was immediate and violent. His body rebelled against the intrusion, wracking him with a fit of coughing that left him doubled over, eyes watering. Yet, beneath the discomfort, something else stirred – a warmth that spread through his chest, a lightness that seemed to lift the weight of his troubles.

By the third puff, Dhruv began to feel... different. The coughing subsided. The ache of his bruises seemed to recede, becoming distant and unimportant. Dhruv felt the tension leave his small body for the first time in longer than he could remember.

Dhruv straightened, blinking in wonder at the world around him. The grimy walls of the alley seemed less oppressive, the distant sounds of the bustling street muffled and inconsequential. He allowed himself a small, secret smile for the first time in what felt like an eternity.

The bidi continued to burn down quickly, its ember a bright point in the gathering dusk. Dhruv savoured each drag, feeling the tension in his muscles slowly uncoil. The constant, gnawing fear that had taken up residence in the pit of his stomach retreated, replaced by a hazy sense of calm.

He looked up at the night sky, marvelling at how the stars seemed brighter, how the cool breeze against his skin felt more vivid. Was this how normal people felt all the time? This sense of calm, of being present in the moment instead of constantly braced for the next blow?

Reality began to creep back in as the bidi burned down to a stub. Dhruv knew he had to return home before his father woke and noticed his absence. But now he had a secret, a small flame of hope to carry with him.

"Thank you, uncle," Dhruv said softly, meeting the kind man's eyes for the first time.

The man nodded, a sad smile on his face. "Be careful, little one. These things can be a friend, but they can also be a trap." Dhruv didn't understand what the man meant, but he nodded anyway.

As he walked home, his steps were lighter than they had been in months. The familiar dread that usually accompanied his return was dulled, pushed to the edges of his consciousness by the lingering effects of the tobacco.

He slipped through the front door, bracing himself for the usual barrage of insults or worse. But tonight, the small apartment was mercifully quiet. His father, Ram, was passed out on the worn sofa, an empty bottle lying on the floor beside him.

Dhruv crept past, holding his breath until he reached the relative safety of his corner. As he curled up on his thin mattress, he inhaled deeply and pressed his face into the pillow. The scent of bidis clung to his clothes and hair, a secret talisman against the night's terrors.

For the first time in months, sleep came easily, unmarred by the usual nightmares. In his dreams, Dhruv floated on a cloud of smoke, far above the reach of belts and angry fists.

What Dhruv didn't realize, couldn't realize at his young age, was that he had just taken the first step down a long and treacherous path. The momentary relief offered by the bidi would soon become a crutch, a necessity rather than a comfort. But for now, all he knew was that he had found a small piece of peace in his turbulent world.

Dhruv's secret affair with bidis deepened. He quickly learned where to find them and how to scrounge enough coins to buy a few sticks at a time. The corner shop owner, a wizened old man with cataracts clouding his eyes, never questioned why a boy of eleven was purchasing bidis. In their neighbourhood, childhood often ended far too soon.

The alley became his sanctuary, where he could breathe – ironic, given that the smoke now filled his lungs increasingly. He learned to roll his own bidis, fingers growing deft at the task. The familiar motions became a comfort in themselves, a moment of focus that pushed away the chaos of his life.

Dhruv became an expert at finding hidden moments, stolen pockets of time where he could indulge in his newfound solace. Early mornings before his father woke, late nights after Ram had drunk himself into a stupor, lunch breaks at the school he still occasionally attended – any opportunity was seized upon with the desperation of a drowning man grasping at a lifeline.

At home, Dhruv and his father's dynamic shifted subtly. Ram's abuse didn't lessen – if anything, his frustration with life seemed to grow with each passing day, and Dhruv remained his primary outlet. But now, Dhruv had a secret weapon, a way to disconnect from the pain and fear that had once consumed him. When his father's mood darkened, signalling the approach of another storm of violence, Dhruv retreated into the hazy cocoon of tobacco-induced calm.

One particularly brutal evening, as Ram's belt whistled through the air, Dhruv retreated into the hazy comfort of his bidi-induced calm. The blows still fell, leaving angry red welts across his back, but the usual overwhelming terror didn't come. Instead, he thought of the bidi waiting for him, the promise of relief just hours away. At that moment, a realisation struck him – the bidis had given him a power his father could never take away, a sense of control in the face of his father's violence.

"You worthless piece of garbage!" Ram roared, his words slurring together. "Just like your mother, always disappointing me!"

In the past, mentioning his absent mother would have reduced Dhruv to tears. Now, he waited for the storm to pass, his mind already on the bidi hidden beneath a loose floorboard in his room.

When Ram finally stumbled away, collapsing onto his bed in a drunken heap, Dhruv didn't immediately reach for his hidden stash as usual. Instead, he sat in the darkness, pondering this new ability to detach, to endure. It wasn't happiness – Dhruv wasn't sure he even remembered what true happiness felt like – but it was... survivable.

The next morning, Dhruv examined his reflection in a cracked mirror. Purple and yellow mottled his skin, a canvas of abuse that would have once sent him spiralling into despair. Now, he reached for a bidi, watching through a haze of smoke as the boy in the mirror transformed. The bruises seemed to fade with each inhale, not physically, but in importance.

As the weeks wore on, his world narrowed, focusing more and more on the next opportunity to smoke. He began to hoard small coins and bills, scrounging what he could from the streets or pilfering from his father's pockets when the man was too far gone to notice. Every rupee was measured in bidis, in moments of escape.

The physical effects of regular bidi use began to manifest, though Dhruv was too young and too focused on his immediate comfort to notice. A persistent cough that he couldn't quite shake, a pallor to his skin that spoke of too little sunlight and too much smoke. His appetite waned, food losing appeal compared to the sharp bite of tobacco on his tongue. But these seemed small prices to pay for the moments of peace the bidis provided.

Yet, even as his body weakened, Dhruv found a strange strength in his addiction. A detached numbness replaced the fear that had once paralysed him in his father's presence. Ram's drunken rages, the crack of the belt against the flesh – these things still happened, but they seemed to be happening to someone else, to a Dhruv who existed just beyond the veil of smoke.

The school became an increasingly distant memory. Dhruv still went through the motions, showing up often enough to avoid immediate suspicion, but his mind was elsewhere. He spent classes in a fog, barely registering the concerned glances of teachers or the whispers of classmates.

Dhruv's teachers noticed the change in him. Once a bright, if quiet, student, he now spent his days in a fog, barely engaging with lessons. His attendance became sporadic, and the smell of tobacco clung to his clothes when he did show up.

Ms. Sharma, his English teacher, tried to reach out. "Dhruv," she said one day, keeping him back after class. "Is everything alright at home? You know you can talk to me if you need help."

Dhruv avoided her concerned gaze, mumbling a noncommittal response. What could he say? Bidis were the only thing keeping him from falling apart completely? He wasn't sure he could face another day in his father's house without them. She wouldn't understand. No one could understand.

After school, he went to the corner shop for his usual supply. For some reason, he wanted to try cigarettes like his father. And before he could ask for one, a well-dressed man entered, asking for a pack of cigarettes. Dhruv watched as the man handed over a crisp hundred-rupee note, receiving only a small amount of change in return. The reality of his situation hit him then – cigarettes were a luxury far beyond his means. Bidis were the only option available to a penniless child like him.

Moreover, bidis were everywhere in his neighbourhood. Men gathered on street corners to share them, shopkeepers kept them within easy reach, and some of the older boys at school traded them in secretive exchanges. They were as much a part of the landscape as the crumbling houses and overflowing gutters.

For Dhruv, bidis represented more than just a cheap substitute for cigarettes. They were a connection to the adult world, a silent rebellion against the powerlessness of his situation. Each puff was an act of defiance, asserting some small measure of control over his life.

As Dhruv left the shop, his precious bidis were tucked safely in his pocket. He was engulfed in a whirlwind of emotions, a mix he couldn't quite decipher. There was the usual anticipation of the calm that would soon envelop him, but there was also a growing realization that this habit, this crutch, was altering him in ways he couldn't fully comprehend.

But understanding was a luxury Dhruv couldn't afford. All he knew was that bidis made the unbearable bearable, and for now, that was enough.

Months passed, and Dhruv's world continued to shrink, narrowing down to the space between one bidi and the next. His young mind, still developing and vulnerable, became increasingly dependent on the false sense of security that tobacco provided. What had once been a novelty, a momentary escape, had become essential to his existence. He measured his life not in hours or days but in the spaces between smokes. The smoke became his armour, each inhale forging a wall between him and the vulnerability of his skin. He didn't have the words to describe what was happening to him – addiction was a concept far beyond his eleven years – but he felt the pull of the bidis growing stronger with each passing day.

The atmosphere remained tense at home, a powder keg always on the verge of explosion. Ram's moods swung wildly, his periods of drunken rage interspersed with moments of maudlin self-pity. Dhruv learned to navigate these choppy waters with the help of his ever-present bidis, using them as a shield against his father's unpredictable behaviour.

One sweltering afternoon, Dhruv returned home to find Ram in one of his rare sober moments. His father sat at their small table, head in his hands, looking older and more defeated than Dhruv had ever seen him.

"Dhruv," Ram said, his voice lacking its usual edge of anger. "Come here, boy."

Dhruv approached cautiously, his body tense, ready to bolt at the first sign of danger. But Ram didn't lash out. Instead, he looked at his son with red-rimmed eyes, a flicker of something – regret? shame? – crossing his face. Dhruv's fear, like a tangible thing, wrapped around him, making him feel small and insignificant.

"You look more like her every day," Ram said softly, almost to himself. "Your mother, she had that same look in her eyes. Like she was always somewhere else, even when she was right in front of me."

Dhruv stood frozen, hardly daring to breathe. His father rarely spoke of his mother and never without anger. This quiet melancholy was new and unsettling. Dhruv's mind was a whirlwind of confusion, unable to process this new side of his father.

"I didn't mean for it to be like this," Ram continued, his words slurring slightly despite his apparent sobriety. "When she left... I just... I couldn't..."

He trailed off, lost in memories or regrets Dhruv couldn't understand. The moment stretched, heavy with unspoken words and years of pain.

Then, as quickly as it had come, the moment passed. Ram's face hardened, the vulnerability replaced by his usual mask of anger and resentment. "What are you staring at, boy? Get out of my sight!"

Dhruv retreated to his corner, his mind reeling. For a brief instant, he had glimpsed something in his father that he had never seen before – a hint of the man Ram might have been before life and loss and alcohol had twisted him into the monster that haunted Dhruv's days and nights.

As the familiar sounds of Ram opening another bottle filled the small apartment, Dhruv reached for a bidi with trembling hands. He needed its comforting haze now more than ever. He needed to blur the edges of this new, confusing reality.

The incident marked a subtle shift in Dhruv's perception of his father. The unassailable figure of terror began to crack, revealing glimpses of a broken man underneath. This didn't make Ram's abuse any less painful or frightening, but it added a layer of complexity that Dhruv's young mind struggled to process.

In the weeks that followed, Dhruv found himself smoking more than ever. Once a source of occasional comfort, the bidis became a constant necessity. He needed them to face his father, to sit through the classes he still occasionally attended, to fall asleep at night with the sounds of Ram's drunken mutterings filtering through the thin walls.

Dhruv's body began to show the strain of his habit. Always small for his age, he now appeared almost wraith-like, his clothes hanging off his bony frame. Dark circles permanently ringed his eyes, and his skin took on a sallow, unhealthy pallor. The persistent cough that had started as a minor irritation became deeper and more troubling.

But Dhruv paid little attention to these physical changes. In his mind, the bidis were still his saviours, the only thing standing between him and complete despair. He couldn't see – or perhaps didn't want to see – how his dependence was slowly poisoning him, stunting not just his body but his potential for a life beyond the cycles of abuse and addiction.

One day, as Dhruv huddled in his usual spot behind the school, savouring a stolen moment with his bidi, he was startled by the appearance of Amit, a classmate he vaguely remembered from the days when he still paid attention in class.

Amit's eyes widened at the sight of the bidi in Dhruv's hand. "Hey, isn't that... are you smoking?"

Dhruv tensed, prepared for judgment or mockery. But Amit's face showed only curiosity, perhaps tinged with admiration.

"Can I try?" Amit asked, glancing around to ensure no teachers were nearby.

For a moment, Dhruv hesitated. A small voice in the back of his mind whispered that he shouldn't pull someone else into the hazy world he now inhabited. But the more significant part of him, which craved connection and validation, won out.

With a slight nod, Dhruv handed over the bidi. He watched Amit take a tentative puff, coughing and sputtering just as Dhruv had done all those months ago. A strange feeling washed over Dhruv – a mix of pride at being the "experienced" one and a deep, aching sadness he couldn't quite explain.

As Amit handed back the bidi, still coughing, he looked at Dhruv with newfound respect. "That's intense," he said. "How do you do it?"

Dhruv shrugged, taking another drag. "You get used to it," he said, his voice raspier than he remembered. "It helps... with things."

Amit nodded, though Dhruv could see he didn't understand. How could he? Amit, with his clean clothes and unmarked skin, couldn't begin to comprehend the demons Dhruv faced daily.

Amit returned to class as they parted ways while Dhruv decided to skip the rest of the day. Dhruv felt a renewed sense of isolation. The bidis, his constant companions, now seemed to emphasise the gulf between him and his peers. He was walking a path that few could understand, let alone follow.

Dhruv wandered the streets, his mind a whirlpool of conflicting emotions. The incident with Amit had stirred something in him, a vague realisation that perhaps his reliance on bidis wasn't as normal or harmless as he'd convinced himself it was. But the thought of facing his life without them was too terrifying to contemplate.

As the sun began to set, casting long shadows across the narrow alleys, Dhruv was drawn back to where he'd first been offered a bidi. The kind-faced uncle wasn't there, but a group of men had gathered, passing around bidis and bottles of cut-rate liquor.

One of the men noticed Dhruv hovering at the edge of the circle. "Aye, little matchstick!" he called out, his words slightly slurred. "Come join us!"

Dhruv hesitated, his instincts warning him to keep his distance. But the promise of more bidis, of prolonging the numbing haze that kept his fears at bay, proved too strong to resist. He stepped forward, accepting a bidi from one of the men with a mumbled thanks.

As he inhaled the familiar harsh smoke, Dhruv felt the tension in his body begin to ease. The men around him laughed and joked, their voices growing louder as the bottles were passed around. In their inebriated state, they seemed to forget that Dhruv was just a child, including him in their adult conversations and crude jokes.

For a brief, intoxicating moment, Dhruv felt a sense of belonging. He wasn't a victim or a burden in this circle of smoke and shared escape. He was just another soul seeking refuge from life's hardships.

CHAPTER FIVE

Breaking Point

The belt whistled through the air, a familiar sound that sent shivers down Dhruv's spine. He braced himself for the impact, his muscles tensing involuntarily. The leather bit into his flesh, and he bit his lip to keep from crying out. He wouldn't give his father the satisfaction.

"Worthless boy!" Ram's words slurred together. His breath reeked of cheap booze. "Can't even pass your exams. What good are you?"

Dhruv wanted to shout back, to tell his father about the long nights he'd spent studying, about how hard he'd tried. But he knew better. Words only made things worse.

Another lash, more brutal this time. Dhruv's vision blurred, tears welling up despite his best efforts. The pain was excruciating, each blow feeling like it was tearing his skin apart.

And then, suddenly, there was a different sound—a sharp crack, followed by a surprised grunt from Ram. Dhruv glanced over his shoulder and saw his father staring dumbfounded at the broken belt in his hands.

For a moment, time seemed to stand still. Dhruv could hear his ragged breathing and could feel the warm trickle of blood down his back. And in that suspended moment, something inside him snapped.

He ran.

Out of the dingy living room, past the rickety kitchen table still littered with empty bottles, through the front door that hung askew on its hinges. He ran, ignoring the burning pain in his back and the ache in his feet as they slapped against the hard-packed earth.

The night air was cool against his skin, carrying the scent of jasmine from somewhere nearby. Dhruv gulped it down greedily, filling his lungs with air that didn't reek of alcohol and failure.

He had no plan, no destination in mind. All he knew was that he couldn't go back. Not this time. Not ever.

As the adrenaline faded, the reality of his situation started to sink in. In the middle of the night, he was alone, with nothing but the clothes on his back. Fear clawed at his throat, threatening to overwhelm him.

But then he remembered the whispers he'd heard at school—hushed conversations about a place where kids like him could go. A shelter, they'd called it. Somewhere safe.

With trembling hands, he fished the crumpled paper from his pocket. The address was smudged, barely legible, but it was all he had.

The streets were eerily quiet as Dhruv made his way through the city. Every shadow made him jump. Every distant sound had him looking over his shoulder. But he pressed on, driven by a desperate hope that somewhere, somehow, things could be different.

It was nothing like he'd imagined when he finally arrived at the youth shelter. No grand building, no flashing neon sign proclaiming safety. Just a modest structure with peeling paint and a small, handwritten sign by the door.

Dhruv hesitated, his hand hovering over the doorbell. What if they turned him away? What if they called his father? What if—

The door opened before he could press the bell, startling him. A woman stood there, her eyes kind but alert. She took in his dishevelled appearance, the way he cradled his arm protectively against his body, the fear in his eyes.

"Come in," she said softly, stepping aside. "You're safe here."

Dhruv hesitated for just a moment longer before stepping inside. The door closed behind him with a soft click, and he felt like he could breathe for the first time in years.

The woman introduced herself as Sunita, a social worker at the shelter. She didn't push for details, didn't demand explanations. Instead, she offered him a warm meal and a place to rest. As she led Dhruv to a small room, Sunita's mind raced, recognising the signs of abuse she'd seen far too many times before. The way Dhruv flinched at sudden movements, how his eyes darted around, always looking for the nearest exit, painted a painfully familiar picture.

"Let's get you settled in," Sunita said, guiding Dhruv to a small room. "We can talk more in the morning after you've had some rest."

Dhruv nodded, unable to form words. The simple kindness in Sunita's voice threatened to unravel the fragile control he'd maintained since fleeing his home.

As Sunita closed the door, leaving Dhruv to rest, she leaned against the wall, taking a deep breath. Cases like this always hit her hard, stirring up memories of her childhood in Patna, of the neighbours whose screams she'd pretended not to hear. She shook her head, pushing the thoughts away.

As Dhruv sank into the narrow bed later that night, his body aching but his belly full, he allowed himself to hope. Maybe, just maybe, this could be a new beginning.

But as he drifted off to sleep, his father's words still rang in his ears. "Worthless boy," they whispered. "What good are you?"

Dhruv squeezed his eyes shut, trying to block out the voices. Tomorrow, he promised himself. Tomorrow, he would start to find out.

The morning light filtered through the thin curtains, casting a pale glow across the dormitory. Dhruv blinked awake, momentarily disoriented by the unfamiliar surroundings. The previous night's events came rushing back, and he felt a twinge of panic in his chest.

He sat up slowly, wincing at the pain that radiated across his back. The other beds in the room were empty and neatly made. How long had he slept?

A soft knock at the door made him jump. "Dhruv?" It was Sunita's voice, gentle but clear. "Are you awake? There's breakfast in the kitchen if you're hungry."

Hunger gnawed at his stomach, but anxiety kept him rooted to the spot. What if this was all a trick? What if his father was waiting outside?

As if sensing his hesitation, Sunita spoke again. "Take your time. No one will rush you here."

The kindness in her voice was almost too much to bear. Dhruv felt tears prickling at the corners of his eyes and angrily wiped them away. Crying wouldn't help. It never had.

Eventually, the rumbling in his stomach overcame his fear. He made his way to the kitchen, keeping his eyes down, shoulders hunched as if expecting a blow at any moment.

The smell of chai and warm roti filled the air, so different from home's stale, alcohol-tinged atmosphere. A few other kids were seated at a long table, talking quietly.

They glanced up as Dhruv entered but quickly returned to their conversations.

Sunita was by the stove, ladling out portions of steaming daal. She smiled warmly when she saw him.

"Good morning, Dhruv," she said, her voice light. "Did you sleep well?"

Dhruv shrugged, his gaze dropping to the floor. "It was... quiet," he mumbled.

Sunita nodded, understanding the unspoken words. Quiet, without the fear of a drunken rage erupting at any moment. "That's good," she said. "Are you hungry? We've got some warm rotis, rice, sabji and daal. Help yourself to whatever you'd like."

He hesitated, unused to such freedom. At home, meals were a battleground, each morsel a potential trigger for his father's rage.

"It's okay," Sunita reassured him, her voice low. "You're safe here. No one will hurt you."

Dhruv nodded, not trusting himself to speak. He filled a plate with shaking hands and retreated to a corner of the table, away from the other kids.

As Dhruv ate, Sunita watched him with a practised eye. She noticed how he hunched over his plate and how his eyes darted around the room. In her mind, she was already formulating a plan to help him, drawing on years of experience and her healing journey.

After breakfast, Sunita asked if he'd like to talk. Dhruv tensed up immediately, but she was quick to reassure him.

"We don't have to discuss anything you're uncomfortable with," she said. "I just want to explain how things work here and maybe get to know you better. Is that okay?"

Dhruv nodded hesitantly. They moved to a small office, cluttered but cosy. Sunita sat behind the desk, gesturing for Dhruv to sit opposite her.

"First things first," she began, her tone gentle but matter-of-fact. "You're not in any trouble. This is a safe place for young people who need help. You can stay here as long as you need to."

Dhruv's eyes widened in disbelief. "Really?" The word slipped out before he could stop it, his voice hoarse from disuse.

Sunita nodded. "Really. We have resources to help you – food, shelter, and medical care. When you're ready, we can also assist with education and job training."

It sounded too good to be true. Dhruv waited for the catch when she'd demand something in return. But Sunita continued explaining the shelter's programs and rules, her voice steady and reassuring.

"Do you have any questions?" she asked when she'd finished.

Dhruv shook his head, overwhelmed by the information and the unexpected kindness.

"That's okay," Sunita said with a smile. "It's a lot to take in. Just remember, you're safe here. No one will force you to do anything you're uncomfortable with."

As Dhruv left the office, he felt a strange lightness in his chest. For the first time in years, he dared to think that maybe, just maybe, things could get better.

The days that followed were a blur of new experiences. Dhruv slowly began to adjust to life at the shelter. He learned the routines, the meal times, the quiet hours. He watched the other kids, marvelling at how easily they seemed to interact, laugh, and just... be.

However, the relative peace of the shelter did not quell the cravings that gnawed at Dhruv. The scent of wood smoke from nearby homes, the sight of men huddled on street corners sharing bidis – these everyday occurrences sent pangs of longing through him. The urge to escape into that familiar haze, to find solace in the burn of tobacco, was a constant battle. He'd traded his father's fists for a different kind of torment, a relentless hunger that no amount of food or sleep could satisfy.

Sunita was a constant presence, always ready with a kind word or a gentle nudge of encouragement. She never pushed Dhruv to talk about his past, but she was always there if he needed someone to listen.

During one of these quiet moments, about a few weeks after his arrival, Dhruv finally found the courage to speak.

"I... I need to stop smoking," Dhruv mumbled, shame colouring his cheeks as he avoided Sunita's gaze while fighting the urge to chase away the anxious thoughts with a familiar burn with his every might.

Sunita placed a comforting hand on his arm. "It's alright, Dhruv," she said, her voice soothing. "It's not easy to break free from something that's been a part of your life for so long." She noticed his hands trembling slightly and offered him a small pack of gum. "Try this. It might help."

Dhruv accepted the gum with a hesitant nod. The minty squares were a poor substitute for the harsh satisfaction of a bidi. Yet, as he unwrapped a piece and popped it into his mouth, a wave of relief washed over him. It helped take the edge off, providing a small measure of relief as he wrestled with the emotional and psychological demons that still haunted him.

As the days turned into weeks, Dhruv began to notice small changes in himself. He stood a little straighter and spoke a little louder. The constant fear that had been his companion for so long began to recede, replaced by a cautious hope.

But at night, when the shelter was quiet, and the memories crept in, Dhruv would still hear his father's voice. "Worthless boy," it would whisper. "What good are you?"

In those moments, Dhruv would clench his fists and remember Sunita's words. He was taking steps. He was trying to be better.

And for now, that had to be enough.

As the weeks at the shelter turned into months, Dhruv settled into a routine that felt almost... normal. The concept was foreign to him, a luxury he'd never known in the chaos of his father's home. Here, meals came at regular times. Sleep wasn't interrupted by drunken rages. And slowly, ever so, Dhruv began to unfurl from the tight ball of fear and anger he'd become.

Sunita, true to her word, had helped him enrol in a vocational program. Every morning, Dhruv would wake early, dress in the cleanest clothes he owned, and make his way to the local technical college. The first day, his hands had trembled so badly he could barely open the door. But day by day, it got easier.

He threw himself into his studies with a fervour that surprised even him. Electronics had always fascinated him. Even amidst the chaos and fear of his childhood, Dhruv had found moments of fascination and wonder in the workings of everyday objects. Broken radios, flickering light bulbs, his friends' discarded toy cars– these things held a strange allure for him. He would spend hours taking them apart, trying to understand the invisible forces that brought them to life.

Now, he had the chance to learn how they worked. In electronics, cause and effect were clear, rules were absolute, and for a boy yearning for stability and control, that was a powerful draw. Each completed circuit, each problem solved, was a tiny victory against the voice in his head that still whispered "worthless."

But it wasn't all smooth sailing. There were days when the weight of his past felt crushing, when every shadow seemed to hide his father's looming figure. On those days, Dhruv would retreat into himself, skipping meals and classes, huddled in his bed at the shelter.

It was after one such episode that Sunita gently suggested therapy.

"It's not about fixing you, Dhruv," she explained, her voice soft but firm. "You're not broken. It's about giving you tools to deal with what you've been through."

Dhruv had baulked at first. The idea of talking to a stranger about the things he could barely admit to himself seemed impossible. But Sunita was patient, and eventually, Dhruv agreed to try.

The first few sessions were excruciating. Dhruv sat in stony silence, arms crossed, unable to meet his therapist's eyes. Dr. Mehra, a kind-faced woman with salt-and-pepper hair, didn't push. She sat with him, occasionally offering a gentle prompt or observation.

It was during the seventh session that something inside Dhruv finally cracked.

"I don't know who I am without the fear," he blurted out, the words tumbling from him in a rush. "I've been afraid for so long... I don't know how to be anything else."

Dr. Mehra nodded, her eyes warm with understanding. "That's a very common feeling, Dhruv. Fear has been your constant companion, your survival mechanism. Learning to live without it is a process that takes time."

With each session, Dhruv found it a little easier to open up. The words still came haltingly, often accompanied by hot tears of shame or anger. But they came. And with them, a gradual sense of lightness, as if each revealed secret lifted a tiny weight from his shoulders.

As the other boys settled into their bunks each night, Dhruv would pace the dormitory, chewing furiously on the gum, trying to outrun the memories that surfaced in the quiet darkness. The shelter was a sanctuary, yes, but the scars he carried ran deeper than the welts on his back. The therapy sessions helped him confront the trauma and untangle the knots of anger and fear that had been festering for years. But the urge to escape, to find a moment's peace in the haze of smoke, remained a constant temptation. It was a struggle he knew he couldn't win alone, and with each piece of gum, each deep breath, he clung to the hope that he could learn to live without the crutch of addiction.

In one of the sessions, Dr Mehra noticed that Dhruv was fidgeting during their session, his leg bouncing nervously, and his fingers constantly picking at a loose thread on his shirt. "You seem a bit on edge today, Dhruv," she observed gently. Dhruv hesitated, then admitted, "I saw someone smoking on my way here. It brought back... the cravings." Dr. Mehra nodded, her expression encouraging. "And what did you do with those cravings?" she asked.

Dhruv took a deep breath. "I kept walking," he said, a hint of pride in his voice. "I remembered what we talked about – the triggers, the coping mechanisms. I used the breathing exercises you taught me." Dr. Mehra smiled warmly. "That's wonderful to hear, Dhruv," she said. "It's a testament to your progress that you could recognise the trigger, acknowledge the craving, and choose a healthier response. Every time you do that, you strengthen your resilience."

Meanwhile, his progress in the vocational program continued. Dhruv's instructors noted his dedication and his quick mind. When they praised his work, Dhruv felt a warmth in his chest that was entirely new. Pride. He was good at something. He was learning, improving, growing.

It was Sunita who suggested he apply for a part-time job at the local grocery store. The idea terrified him – interacting with strangers, handling money, and the possibility of making mistakes. But Sunita believed in him, and slowly, Dhruv was learning to believe in himself, too.

"You're capable of more than you know, Dhruv," Sunita said, her voice filled with quiet conviction. "This job is just one step. You've already come so far."

His first shift was a nightmare of anxiety. His hands shook as he bagged groceries, convinced that at any moment he would drop something, break something, prove himself the failure his father had always said he was. But the hours ticked by, and nothing terrible happened. Customers smiled at him. His co-workers were patient with his mistakes. And at the end of the day, his manager patted him on the back and said, "Good job, kid."

Dhruv walked back to the shelter that evening in a daze. Good job. When was the last time anyone had said that to him? Had anyone ever said that to him?

That night, as he lay in his bed at the shelter, Dhruv found himself thinking about the future for the first time in years. Not in terms of survival, of getting through the next day or week, but in terms of possibilities. What if he finished the vocational program? What if he could get a full-time job? What if...

The thought trailed off, too big and bright to fully contemplate. But it was there, a tiny spark of hope in the darkness.

During his therapy session the following day, Dhruv finally found the words to articulate the change he felt stirring inside him.

"I want to be better," he said, his voice barely above a whisper. "Better than him. I want to break this... this cycle."

Dr. Mehra nodded, a gentle smile on her face. "That's a powerful goal, Dhruv. And you've already taken the first steps towards it."

Those words became a lifeline for Dhruv, a mantra he repeated to himself in moments of doubt. Better. He could be better.

The path ahead was still long and uncertain. There were still nights when he woke in a cold sweat, his father's voice echoing in his ears. There were still days when the most straightforward tasks seemed insurmountable, when the urge to run and hide nearly overwhelmed him.

But there were also moments of unexpected joy. The satisfaction of solving a complex problem in class. The warmth of sharing a joke with his co-workers. The simple pleasure of walking down the street without constantly looking over his shoulder.

Slowly and painfully, Dhruv was learning to live rather than survive. And with each small step forward, the person he could become – the person he wanted to become – seemed a little less impossible.

As he stood at the window of the shelter one evening, watching the sunset over the city, Dhruv allowed himself a small smile. The future was still uncertain, but for the first time in his life, it held more promise than fear.

He wasn't healed. He wasn't "fixed." But he was trying. He was growing. He was step by step becoming better.

And for now, that was enough.

As the seasons changed, so did Dhruv. The timid boy who had arrived at the shelter months ago slowly gave way to a young man who walked with purpose, dared to meet people's eyes, and occasionally even smiled.

His progress in the vocational program continued to impress his instructors. Dhruv found himself drawn to the intricacies of circuit design, losing himself for hours in the delicate dance of electrons and resistors. During one of these sessions, he experienced a moment of pure, unadulterated joy – a feeling so foreign that it almost scared him.

He had been working on a particularly challenging project, a complex circuit that had stumped even some of his classmates. For days, he had pored over diagrams, double-checking connections, trying to understand why the circuit refused to work. And then, in a moment of clarity, he saw it. A tiny error, a misplaced resistor, changed everything.

With trembling hands, he corrected. The circuit hummed to life, lights blinking in perfect sequence. Dhruv stared at it, barely daring to breathe. He had done it. He had solved the puzzle.

The rush of pride and accomplishment that followed was unlike anything he had ever experienced. For a brief, shining moment, his father's voice was utterly silent, drowned out by the thrill of success.

But life, Dhruv was learning, was rarely a straight path forward. For every triumph, there seemed to be a setback waiting just around the corner.

It happened on a crisp autumn afternoon. Dhruv was working his shift at the grocery store, restocking shelves with a quiet efficiency that had become his trademark. The repetitive task was almost meditative, allowing his mind to wander to his latest electronics project.

And then he heard a crash, followed by a man's angry shout.

"You clumsy idiot! Look what you've done!"

The words, so achingly familiar, sent Dhruv spiralling. In an instant, he was a child again, cowering before his father's rage. The can of beans in his hand clattered to the floor as he stumbled backwards, his breath coming in short, panicked gasps.

He was vaguely aware of concerned voices, of gentle hands, trying to guide him. But all he could hear was his father's voice; all he could see was the raised belt whistling through the air.

Dhruv didn't remember leaving the store. His next clear memory was of sitting on a bench in a nearby park, Sunita's calm voice gradually penetrating the fog of panic.

"Breathe, Dhruv," she was saying. "You're safe. You're not there anymore. Breathe with me."

Slowly, painfully, Dhruv clawed his way back to the present. The park came into focus – the rustle of leaves, the distant laughter of children, the warmth of the sun on his face. Real. This was real. Not the nightmare of his past.

Shame washed over him as the full impact of what had happened hit home. He had run from his job. He had caused a scene. All his progress and one angry voice had been enough to undo it all.

"I'm sorry, Di", he whispered, unable to meet Sunita's eyes. "I've ruined everything."

But Sunita's voice was gentle, free of the judgment Dhruv expected. "You haven't ruined anything, Dhruv. What you experienced was a panic attack. It's a normal response to trauma. It doesn't erase all the progress you've made."

Over the next few days, Dhruv struggled to believe her. He was sure he'd be fired and kicked out of his vocational program. But to his amazement, that didn't happen. His manager at the store was understanding, even concerned. His instructors offered support, not condemnation.

The incident became a turning point in Dhruv's therapy. With Dr. Mehra's guidance, he began to delve deeper into his trauma to confront the fears that still held him captive.

"Healing isn't linear," Dr. Mehra reminded him gently. "There will be setbacks. But each time you face your fears and choose to move forward despite them, you grow stronger."

Slowly, Dhruv began to internalise this truth. The panic attacks didn't disappear entirely, but he learned strategies to manage them. Breathing exercises, grounding techniques, positive self-talk – tools that helped him navigate the stormy seas of his emotions.

A chill wind whistled through the streets of Patna, carrying the scent of wood smoke and the promise of winter. The warmth cocooned Dhruv inside the shelter as he sat across from Sunita. She was about to start a conversation Dhruv wasn't sure he was ready for.

Sunita's voice, as gentle as ever, broke the silence. "Have you thought about what you'd like to do once you leave the shelter?"

Dhruv's eyes darted around the room—the worn couch where they'd had so many of these talks, the bulletin board crowded with photos of past and present residents. All these reminders of the stability he'd fought so hard to build made his stomach twist. He shifted in his seat, unsure. "Di," he began, his voice low, hesitant.

Sunita leaned forward slightly, her tone soft yet firm. "Dhruv, you've come so far. You've worked hard, healed, and built a solid foundation. It's time to take the next step."

Dhruv's heart pounded in his chest. Sensing his unease, Sunita's eyes softened. "Leaving doesn't mean you're alone," she reassured him, her voice warm and steady. "I'll still be here every step of the way."

The prospect of leaving the safety of the shelter terrified him. But a small part of him, a part that grew stronger each day, was excited by the possibility. A place of his own. A life of his own making.

With Sunita's help, he began to plan. His savings from the grocery store job and a small stipend from a support program for at-risk youth would be enough for a tiny studio apartment. It would be cramped in a less-than-ideal neighbourhood, but it would be his.

As the day of his departure from the shelter approached, Dhruv found himself reflecting on how far he had come. He was not whole, not yet. The scars of his past still ached, the voice of his father still whispered in moments of doubt, and cravings still gnawed at him. But he was stronger now. He had the tools to fight back. He had people who believed in him.

Most importantly, he was beginning to believe in himself.

On his last night at the shelter, Dhruv stood at the window, looking at the city. Sunita approached quietly, standing beside him.

"You've come a long way, Dhruv," she said softly.

Dhruv nodded, his eyes still on the twinkling lights outside. "I couldn't have done it without you, Di," he said. "Without this place."

Sunita smiled, feeling a mix of pride and bittersweetness. This was the hardest part of her job – saying goodbye. But it was also the most rewarding. "You did the hard work, Dhruv. We just provided the space for you to do it."

As Dhruv turned from the window, he caught sight of his reflection in the glass. He thought he saw his father's face staring back at him for a moment. But then he blinked, and it was just him. Dhruv. Scarred but standing. Afraid but moving forward.

"I will be better," he whispered to his reflection. "I am better."

And for the first time, he truly believed it.

Sunita watched him, her heart full. In Dhruv's journey, she saw echoes of her past; in his resilience, she saw hope for the future. This was why she did this work – to help break the cycle, one child at a time.

CHAPTER SIX

Building

The studio apartment was smaller than Dhruv had imagined, barely larger than his room at the shelter. A single window let in a sliver of sunlight, illuminating the peeling wallpaper and weathered concrete floor. But as Dhruv stood in the doorway, a small duffel bag containing all his worldly possessions at his feet, he felt a surge of something he couldn't quite name. Pride? Anxiety? Hope? Perhaps all three, swirling together in a cocktail of emotion that left him dizzy.

"Home," he whispered, testing the word on his tongue. It felt foreign, dangerous almost. Home had always been a place of fear, of pain. Could he make it something different?

The first few nights were the hardest. The silence was oppressive, broken only by the occasional rumble of traffic outside and the steady drip of a leaky faucet he hadn't yet figured out how to fix. Dhruv found himself lying awake, staring at the cracked ceiling, his mind racing with doubts and fears.

What if he couldn't do this? What if he failed? What if his father had been right all along, and he was worthless?

In those dark hours, Dhruv clung to the techniques Dr. Mehra had taught him. Deep breaths. Grounding exercises. Positive affirmations that felt hollow at first but gradually began to take root.

"I am capable. I am worthy. I am more than my past."

The urge to smoke was a constant battle, but Dhruv fought it with every fibre of his being. Each time he resisted the temptation and chose a healthier coping mechanism, he felt a surge of pride, a reinforcement of his commitment to a better life.

Slowly, day by day, Dhruv began to settle into a routine. Mornings were for his vocational program and afternoons for his job at the grocery store. Evenings were spent tinkering with electronic projects or studying for his upcoming certification exam.

He still met with Sunita once weekly, now in her office at the shelter rather than across the breakfast table. Her steady presence was an anchor, reminding him how far he'd come even when he felt adrift.

"Remember, Dhruv," she'd say, her eyes kind but firm, "independence doesn't mean you have to do everything alone. Asking for help when you need it is a sign of strength, not weakness."

It was a lesson Dhruv struggled with. Years of self-reliance, of knowing that showing vulnerability would only invite more pain, were hard to unlearn. But he was trying.

The first time he invited a classmate over to study, Dhruv spent hours frantically cleaning his tiny apartment, terrified of judgment. But Raj, a fellow electronics enthusiast with a quick smile and quicker wit, didn't notice the shabby furniture or the water stain on the ceiling.

"Nice setup," Raj said, nodding at the cluttered desk where Dhruv had his latest project spread out. "Is that the advanced circuit design you were talking about in class?"

And just like that, they were deep into the conversation about resistors and capacitors. The awkwardness was forgotten. Raj casually suggested they make it a regular thing as he left hours later. Dhruv found himself nodding, a small smile tugging at his lips.

It wasn't all smooth sailing, of course. There were still days when the weight of his past felt crushing, when the most straightforward tasks seemed insurmountable. The panic attacks hadn't disappeared entirely, though they were less frequent now.

One awful day, Dhruv found himself huddled in the corner of his apartment, tears streaming down his face as he struggled to breathe. In desperation, he fumbled for his phone and dialled Sunita's number.

"I can't do this, Di", he gasped when she answered. "It's too much. I'm not strong enough."

Sunita's voice was calm, steady. "Breathe with me, Dhruv. That's it. In and out. You are strong enough. You've proven that time and time again. This feeling will pass."

And it did. Slowly, painfully, but it passed. When Dhruv finally uncurled from his defensive posture, muscles aching, and eyes swollen, he felt a flicker of pride beneath the exhaustion. He had faced the storm and came out the other side. He had asked for help when he needed it.

As the weeks turned into months, Dhruv's apartment began to feel more like home. He hung a few posters on the walls – circuit diagrams that were as beautiful as any art to him. A small potted plant, a gift from Raj, sat on the windowsill, reaching towards the sunlight.

His final project for the vocational program consumed most of his free time. It was ambitious – a small robot designed to navigate obstacles and perform simple tasks. There were moments of frustration when nothing seemed to work when he was tempted to give up. But each small success, each problem solved, fuelled his determination.

The day he presented his project to the class, Dhruv's hands shook so badly he could barely set up his demonstration. But as he explained his design, his voice grew more assertive. This was something he understood, something he had created with his own hands and mind.

When his robot completed its programmed tasks, navigating the obstacle course with smooth precision, the room erupted in applause. Dhruv stood there, stunned, as his classmates and instructors crowded around, asking questions and offering congratulations.

"Exceptional work, Dhruv," his instructor said, clapping him on the shoulder. "You should be very proud."

Proud. The word echoed in Dhruv's mind as he went home that evening. He was proud. Not just of the project but of himself. Of the person he was becoming.

As he unlocked the door to his apartment, Dhruv paused momentarily, taking in the space that had become his sanctuary. It wasn't perfect. The faucet still dripped, and the wallpaper was still peeling in places. But it was his. A place where he felt safe and could grow and dream and become.

Dhruv smiled a genuine smile that reached his eyes. "I'm home," he said softly, and the word felt right this time. It felt like a promise like a future waiting to unfold.

He wasn't healed, not entirely. The scars of his past would always be a part of him. But they no longer defined him. He was Dhruv – a student, worker, and friend. A young man with dreams and fears, strengths and weaknesses. A human being, complex and contradictory and full of potential.

As he settled in for the evening, Dhruv thought about the future again. But this time, it wasn't with fear or uncertainty. It was with cautious optimism and a growing belief in his resilience and capability.

He was on his way. And for the first time in his life, Dhruv was excited to see where the path might lead.

The seasons turned, and with them, Dhruv's life continued to evolve. Spring brought new opportunities, both thrilling and terrifying. His success with the robot project caught the attention of a local tech start-up, TechNova, and they offered him an internship. It was a chance to put his skills to the test in the real world, to see if he could truly make a career out of his passion for electronics.

The night before his first day, Dhruv barely slept. He tossed and turned, his mind racing with a mixture of excitement and anxiety. What if he wasn't good enough? What if he made a fool of himself? What if, what if, what if...

As dawn broke, Dhruv dragged himself out of bed, exhausted but determined. He stood before the small mirror in his bathroom, adjusting the collar of his newly purchased button-up shirt. The face that looked back at him was still young, still carrying the shadows of his past, but there was a strength in his eyes that hadn't been there before.

"You can do this," he told his reflection firmly. "You've come this far. You won't fail now."

TechNova's office was a far cry from anything Dhruv had experienced before. The open-plan space buzzed with energy, people hunched over computers or gathered in small groups, talking animatedly about projects Dhruv could barely comprehend. For a moment, he felt overwhelmed, out of place in this world of innovation and ambition.

But then his supervisor, a woman named Priya with kind eyes and a no-nonsense attitude, was there, guiding him to his workstation and outlining his first tasks. As Dhruv immersed himself in the work, his nervousness faded, replaced by the familiar focus that always came when solving a problem.

The weeks flew by in a whirlwind of new experiences. Dhruv found himself working on projects that challenged him and pushed him to the limits of his knowledge and beyond. There were moments of frustration, times when he felt hopelessly out of his depth. But there were also moments of triumph when a piece of code finally worked, or a circuit design came together perfectly.

Dhruv's co-workers were unlike anyone he had ever met before. They were passionate, driven, and often eccentric in their ways. At first, he kept to himself, still wary of forming connections. But gradually, drawn in by their enthusiasm and genuine interest in his ideas, Dhruv began to open up.

He found an unexpected ally in Arjun, a software developer with a dry sense of humour and a talent for explaining complex concepts in simple terms. Arjun took Dhruv under his wing, offering advice not just on coding but navigating office politics and building a career in tech.

"You've got real talent, kid," Arjun told him one day over lunch. "Don't let anyone make you doubt that, including yourself."

The words stayed with Dhruv, a talisman against the self-doubt that still plagued him in his darker moments.

As his confidence grew at work, Dhruv also found the courage to take on new challenges in his personal life. He joined a support group for survivors of abuse, something he had resisted for months despite Dr. Mehra's gentle encouragement.

The first meeting was one of the hardest things Dhruv had ever done. Sitting in a circle with strangers, expected to bare his soul, he felt exposed and vulnerable in a way that made his skin crawl. But as he listened to others share their stories, he realised something profound: he wasn't alone. The details varied, but the pain, the fear, and the struggle to reclaim their lives were all achingly familiar.

When it came time for Dhruv to speak, he started hesitantly, his voice barely above a whisper. But as the words came, halting at first and then in a rush, he felt something shift inside him. It was as if a weight he hadn't even known he was carrying began to lift.

"I'm not - I'm not the person he tried to make me," Dhruv said, his voice growing stronger. "I'm more than what happened to me. I'm... I'm me."

The simple declaration felt like a revelation. At that moment, surrounded by people who understood, Dhruv felt a sense of belonging he had never experienced before.

As summer approached, bringing sweltering heat that turned the city into a shimmering mirage, Dhruv faced another milestone. His internship was ending, and with it came a decision: TechNova offered him a full-time position.

It was more money than Dhruv had ever dreamed of earning, a chance to establish himself in a career he loved truly. But it also meant more responsibility and higher stakes. The thought of it made his palms sweat and his heart race.

The night before he had to give his answer, Dhruv found himself walking to the youth shelter where his journey had begun. As always, Sunita was ready with a warm smile and a listening ear.

"I'm scared," Dhruv admitted, sitting in her office, which still felt like a haven after all this time. "What if I'm not ready? What if I'm making a mistake?"

Sunita regarded him thoughtfully. "Dhruv, do you remember the boy who came to us that night, battered and terrified? Look how far you've come since then. You've faced your fears. You've worked hard. You've grown in ways I don't think you even realise. You're ready for this. The question is, do you want it?"

Did he want it? Dhruv closed his eyes, picturing the life this job could offer him. Financial security. Professional growth. A chance to create, innovate, and make a difference in the world. Beyond that, he had a chance to prove to himself, once and for all, that he was more than his past.

"Yes," he said, opening his eyes. "Yes, I want it."

The smile that spread across Sunita's face was radiant with pride. "Then go get it, Dhruv. And remember, no matter what happens, you always have a home here."

The following day, Dhruv walked into TechNova's office with his head held high. His hands were steady as he signed the contract, his voice clear as he thanked Priya for the opportunity.

As he settled into his new role, now a full-fledged member of the team, Dhruv felt a sense of possibility that was both exhilarating and terrifying. The future stretched before him, no longer a source of dread but a canvas waiting to be filled.

He wasn't naive enough to think it would be easy. There would be challenges, setbacks, and days when the ghosts of his past would threaten to overwhelm him. But now he had the tools to fight back. He had support. He had strength he never knew he possessed.

Most importantly, he had hope. Hope for a future of his own making, a life defined not by what had been done to him but by what he chose to do.

As Dhruv threw himself into his first project as a full-time employee, he allowed himself a small smile. He was on his way. And for the first time, he couldn't wait to see where the journey would take him.

As autumn painted the city in gold and crimson hues, Dhruv settled into a rhythm he had never thought possible. His days were filled with the challenges and triumphs of his work at the start-up, his evenings with a growing circle of friends or quiet moments of self-reflection. He was, he realised, with a mix of wonder and trepidation, building a life.

But even as he moved forward, the shadows of his past lingered. They crept into his dreams, turning them into nightmares that left him gasping for air. They whispered doubts in quiet moments and tried to undermine every achievement with insidious thoughts of unworthiness.

It was during one of his therapy sessions with Dr. Mehra that Dhruv finally voiced a fear that had been growing in the back of his mind.

"What if I become like him?" he asked, his voice barely above a whisper. "What if... what if the anger, the violence, it's in my blood? What if I can't escape it?"

Dr. Mehra regarded him thoughtfully. "Dhruv, the fact that you're asking these questions and aware of this fear already sets you apart. You're not destined to repeat the cycle of abuse. You have a choice."

"But how can I be sure?" Dhruv pressed, the words tumbling out in a rush. "Sometimes I feel this anger, this rage, and it scares me. What if I can't control it?"

"Anger itself isn't the problem," Dr. Mehra explained gently. "It's a normal human emotion. The problem comes from how we choose to express or act on that anger. You've already shown tremendous control and growth in handling your emotions. But we can work on more specific strategies for managing anger healthily if you'd like."

Over the next few weeks, Dhruv threw himself into this new aspect of his healing journey. He learned breathing techniques to calm himself in moments of frustration. He practised identifying and articulating his feelings before they could build up into uncontrollable anger. He even started a journal, pouring his thoughts and fears onto the pages when they became too much to hold inside.

But the actual test of his progress came on a crisp October evening as Dhruv was leaving work. He was distracted, his mind already on his dinner plans with Raj and some other friends from his vocational program. He didn't notice the man until they collided, Dhruv's shoulder sending the stranger stumbling.

"Watch where you're going, you idiot!" the man snarled, his words slurred with alcohol.

Dhruv froze, his heart pounding. The man's voice. The smell of liquor on his breath. It was all too familiar. For a moment, he was a child again, cowering before his father's rage.

But then, something shifted. Dhruv took a deep breath, centring himself the way Dr. Mehra had taught him. He was not that helpless child anymore. He had choices.

"I'm sorry," Dhruv said, his voice steady. "It was an accident. Are you alright?"

The man blinked, clearly taken aback by the calm response. He muttered something unintelligible and stumbled away, leaving Dhruv standing there, trembling slightly but upright.

It wasn't until he reached his apartment that the full impact of what had happened hit him. He had faced his fear. He had controlled his reaction. He had broken the cycle.

Overwhelmed by emotion, Dhruv sank to the floor, tears streaming down his face. But these were not tears of fear or pain. They were tears of relief, of release, of a profound realisation that his past did not bind him.

When he finally collected himself, Dhruv reached for his phone. His dinner plans were forgotten; he dialled a number he knew by heart.

"Sunita?" he said when she answered. "I... I think I need to talk."

An hour later, Dhruv found himself in Sunita's office at the shelter, pouring out the story of what had happened. Sunita listened attentively, her eyes shining with pride.

"Do you see now, Dhruv?" she asked when he had finished. "Do you see how strong you've become?"

Dhruv nodded, a small smile tugging at his lips. "I'm not him," he said softly. "I never will be."

"No," Sunita agreed. "You're Dhruv. And you're forging your path."

As he left the shelter that night, Dhruv felt lighter than he had in years. The fear of becoming like his father, which had haunted him for so long, began to loosen its grip.

In the following days, Dhruv looked at the world with new eyes. He noticed the small kindnesses people showed each other – a stranger holding a door open, a co-worker bringing coffee to someone having a rough day. He saw how people chose compassion over cruelty and patience over anger.

And he saw himself reflected in the eyes of those who had come to care for him. Raj, who valued his friendship. Arjun, who respected his skills and ideas. Sunita and Dr. Mehra, who had believed in him even when he couldn't believe in himself.

One evening, as Dhruv sat at his small desk, tinkering with a personal project, he caught sight of his reflection on the computer screen. The face that looked back at him was older now, lined with the beginnings of laugh lines and the scars of his past. But the eyes were clear, steady, filled with a quiet determination.

"I am Dhruv," he whispered to his reflection, a declaration and a promise. "I am not defined by what was done to me. I am defined by what I choose to do."

As he turned back to his project, Dhruv felt a sense of peace settle over him. The journey wasn't over – there would always be challenges to face and fears to overcome. But he was ready for them. He had the strength, the tools, and the support to face whatever lay ahead.

For the first time in his life, Dhruv wasn't just surviving. He was living. And the future, once a source of dread, now held the promise of endless possibilities.

The winter brought with it a chill in the air and a new challenge that would test everything Dhruv had learned about himself. TechNova was preparing to launch its first major product, and Dhruv found himself at the centre of a storm of deadlines, debugging sessions, and late nights.

The pressure was intense. Dhruv's role had expanded, and he was now responsible for a critical component of the product's hardware. Each day brought new problems to solve and new obstacles to overcome. There were moments when the old doubts crept in, whispering that he wasn't good enough, that he would fail and prove his father right.

But Dhruv was not the same person he had been. He now had tools and strategies to combat negative thoughts. In the moments when it all felt overwhelming, he would step away from his desk, find a quiet corner, and practice the breathing exercises Dr. Mehra had taught him. He reached out to his support network – Raj for a laugh, Arjun for technical advice, and Sunita for a grounding conversation.

One particularly stressful day, when a critical component refused to work no matter what Dhruv tried, he was on the verge of a breakdown. His hands were shaking, his breath coming in short gasps. For a moment, he was tempted to lash out, to scream in frustration the way his father would have.

Instead, he closed his eyes and took a deep breath. "I am not my father," he whispered to himself. "I can handle this."

Dhruv stood up, stretched, and then did something that surprised even himself. He walked over to Priya's desk.

"I'm struggling with this component," he admitted, his voice steady despite his nerves. "I've tried everything I can think of, but I'm not making progress. I could use some help."

Priya looked up at him, her expression not of disappointment as Dhruv had feared but of understanding. "Thank you for letting me know, Dhruv," she said. "Let's take a look together. Sometimes, a fresh pair of eyes is all we need."

As they worked through the problem together, Dhruv felt a weight lift from his shoulders. He hadn't failed by asking for help; he had shown maturity and professionalism. It was a revelation that would have been unthinkable to Dhruv a year ago.

The launch date loomed closer, and the entire office was a hive of activity. Dhruv found himself working longer hours, fuelled by caffeine and determination. But unlike in the past, when stress would have sent him spiralling into self-doubt and anxiety, he felt a strange sense of exhilaration.

He was pushing himself to his limits, but he was also growing, learning, and proving to himself how much he could achieve. Each solved problem, each successful test, was a small victory that built his confidence.

The night before the launch, Dhruv stayed at the office later than anyone else, running final checks on his component. As he worked, he wondered how far he had come from a terrified boy fleeing an abusive home to a skilled professional on the cusp of launching a product that could change lives. The contrast was so stark it almost made him dizzy.

When he finally left the office in the early morning, the city was quiet, blanketed in a drizzle. Dhruv stood for a moment outside the building, tilting his face up to feel the cool touch of rain on his skin. He felt a profound sense of peace, of rightness. Whatever happened tomorrow, he knew he had given his all. He had faced his fears, pushed through his doubts, and emerged stronger.

Launch day dawned bright and clear. The office was a whirlwind of activity, last-minute checks and nervous energy. Dhruv moved through it all with a calm focus that surprised him. When it was time for the final demonstration, he stood tall, his voice clear as he explained the function of his component.

As the product came to life, working flawlessly, the room erupted in cheers. Dhruv found himself engulfed in hugs and handshakes, words of congratulation washing over him. He caught Priya's eye across the room, and she gave him a nod of approval that filled him with pride.

As the team celebrated their achievement in the aftermath of the successful launch, Dhruv slipped away for a moment of quiet. He was in a small conference room, staring at the city skyline. His reflection in the window looked back at him– a young man with tired eyes but a smile of quiet satisfaction.

"I did it, Baba," he whispered, not to the father who had hurt him but to the father he wished he'd had. The father he might one day become. "I did it."

A soft knock at the door interrupted his reverie. It was Arjun, holding two glasses of champagne.

"There you are," Arjun said. "Quite a day, huh? You should be proud, kid. Your work was crucial to this success."

Dhruv felt a lump form in his throat. "Thank you," he managed. "For everything. Your guidance, your support... it means more than you know."

Arjun clapped him on the shoulder. "You did the hard work, Dhruv. I just pointed you in the right direction. Now come on, the team's waiting to toast our newest rising star."

As Dhruv followed Arjun to the main office, he felt a sense of belonging. This was his team, his accomplishment, his life. He had built this, step by painful step, from the ashes of his past.

The future stretched before him, no longer a source of fear but a canvas of possibilities. There would be more challenges, more moments of doubt, and more obstacles to overcome. But Dhruv was ready for them. He had survived the worst life could throw at him. He had rebuilt himself, stronger and wiser.

As he re-joined the celebration, accepting congratulations and sharing in the joy of his colleagues, Dhruv allowed himself to fully embrace the moment. He was Dhruv- a survivor, friend, and professional. He was whole, he was healing, he was becoming.

And for the first time in his life, that was more than enough. It was everything.

CHAPTER SEVEN

The Dilemma

The hospital corridor stretched out before Dhruv like an endless tunnel, its lights casting a cold, unforgiving glow. The air hung heavy with the scent of disinfectant intertwining with the pervasive undercurrent of anxiety that seemed to saturate every nook and cranny of the hospital.

Each of Dhruv's steps echoed against the polished linoleum, a metronome marking the agonising passage of time. His heart hammered in his chest, a relentless drumbeat that drowned out the hushed murmurs of nurses and the distant beeps of medical equipment. The world around him seemed to blur into a haze of white and blue, the colours of the hospital walls and the nurses' scrubs blending into an indistinct canvas of worry.

Dhruv's mind raced, replaying the events of the past few hours in a relentless loop. Priya's sudden collapse, her hand reaching out to him as her eyes fluttered closed. The frantic drive to the hospital, the blur of nurses and doctors speaking in urgent tones. And now, he found himself in this liminal space between hope and despair, waiting for news that could shatter his world.

As if on cue, the delivery room doors swung open. A nurse emerged, her eyes scanning the corridor before landing on Dhruv. He stood, his heart in his throat, every nerve in his body alight with anticipation.

This was it. The moment everything changed.

A nurse approached, her expression carefully neutral. "Mr. Dhruv?" she said softly, her voice gentle but firm. "If you'll come with me, please."

Dhruv's heart leapt into his throat as he followed her, his legs moving of their own accord. The nurse led him to a small consultation room, its walls adorned with posters of medical procedures and public health announcements. A doctor in rumpled scrubs waited inside, his face etched with lines of fatigue and concern.

"Mr. Dhruv," the doctor began, his voice low and measured. "I'm afraid we're facing a critical situation with your wife and child."

Dhruv nodded mechanically, bracing himself for what was to come. His hands were clammy, and he wiped them surreptitiously on his pants, trying to maintain some semblance of composure.

"Priya is experiencing severe complications," the doctor continued, his eyes filled with compassion. "Her blood pressure has dropped dangerously low, and we're struggling to stabilise her. The baby is also in distress. Her heart rate is erratic and declining."

The words washed over Dhruv like a tide of ice-cold water. He struggled to process their meaning, to comprehend the enormity of what the doctor was saying. His mind felt like a whirlwind, thoughts and emotions churning in a chaotic dance.

"We're doing everything we can," the doctor said, his voice steady but grave. "But I need to be frank with you. We may reach a point where we have to make a choice. We may not be able to save them both."

The room seemed to tilt on its axis. Dhruv gripped the edge of a nearby chair, his knuckles turning white as he fought to maintain his balance. "What... what are you saying?" he choked out, his voice barely above a whisper.

The doctor's eyes were filled with compassion as he explained, "If it comes down to it, we may need to prioritise either Priya or the baby. I know this is an impossible decision, but we must be prepared. We need to know your wishes."

Dhruv's mind reeled. How could he possibly make such a choice? His beloved Priya, the woman who had been his anchor, his salvation, or their unborn daughter, a life full of potential they'd dreamed of for so long? The weight of the decision pressed down on him like a physical force, threatening to crush him.

As the doctor waited patiently, Dhruv's thoughts spiralled. He saw Priya's radiant smile and felt the warmth of her hand in his. He remembered the day they found out she was pregnant, the joy that had bloomed between them like a rare and precious flower. The memory of her laughter echoed in his mind, a sound that had always been able to chase away his darkest thoughts.

But then, unbidden, other memories surfaced. The weight of his father's belt, the sting of cruel words hurled in drunken rages. The suffocating fear that had been his constant companion as a child. The lingering scent of alcohol on his father's breath was a reminder of the violence that could erupt at any moment.

Dhruv closed his eyes, fighting back tears. He imagined a future without Priya, trying to raise their daughter alone. The thought filled him with a paralysing terror. How could he, damaged as he was, possibly give a child the love and security she would need? Wouldn't he just perpetuate the cycle of pain and trauma that had defined his own life?

"Mr. Dhruv?" The doctor's voice pulled him back to the present. "We need to make a decision. The baby's heart rate is dropping, and your wife—"

"Save Priya," Dhruv blurted out, his voice cracking. "Please, save my wife at any cost."

The words hung in the air, heavy with finality. As soon as they left his lips, Dhruv was hit by a wave of guilt so powerful it nearly knocked him off his feet. Had he just sentenced their unborn daughter to an uncertain fate? The thought was like a knife twisting in his gut.

The doctor nodded gravely and disappeared back into the delivery room, leaving Dhruv alone with his thoughts. He slumped against the wall, his legs barely supporting him. His fingers trembled as he reached into his pocket, muscle memory guiding him to the familiar shape of a bidi.

The corridor began to spin, and Dhruv closed his eyes, letting the memories wash over him. He saw Priya on their wedding day, radiant in her red sari, her eyes sparkling with happiness. He heard her laugh, a sound that had always been able to chase away his darkest thoughts. He felt the gentle swell of her belly under his hand, the first time they felt their daughter kick.

And now, in this moment of crisis, he had made his choice. He had chosen to prioritize his fears and inadequacies over their child's life. The weight of this decision was a burden that threatened to crush him.

Dhruv slid down the wall until he was sitting on the cold floor, his head in his hands. Tears streamed down his face as he grappled with the magnitude of his decision. He had always feared becoming like his father, and now, in this moment of ultimate vulnerability, he wondered if he had proven himself to be just as selfish, just as unworthy of love.

The hospital corridor was a symphony of sounds, each a stark reminder of the lives in the balance. The beep of monitors, the soft hum of machinery, the distant murmur of voices. Dhruv sat there, suspended in this limbo, the only sound of his ragged breathing.

Time lost all meaning as he sat there, trapped in a purgatory of his own making.

He remembered the first time he had met Priya and how her smile lit up the room. He remembered their first date. A nervous excitement coursed through him as they walked along the river, their hands brushing against each other.

He remembered the countless nights they had spent talking, sharing their dreams and fears. Priya had been his rock, his confidante, who had seen beyond his pain and believed in him. And now, he had chosen to prioritise her life over their unborn daughter's.

The weight of his decision was a physical ache, a gnawing pain in the pit of his stomach. He wondered if he could ever look at himself in the mirror again to face the reflection of a man who had made such an impossible choice.

The minutes ticked by with agonising slowness. Each passing second felt like an eternity, a stretch of time filled with uncertainty and dread. Dhruv's mind was a whirlwind of thoughts, each more painful than the last.

He thought about the life he and Priya had built together, the love that had blossomed despite their challenges. He thought about the future they had dreamed of, the family they had hoped to create. And now, that future hung in the balance, a fragile dream that could shatter any moment. His heart raced, sweat beading on his forehead. The craving clawed at him, a physical ache that consumed his entire being.

He closed his eyes, trying to steady himself, but the darkness only amplified the desire. In his mind's eye, he could see the packet of bidis and almost feel the familiar weight in his hand. Before he knew what he was doing, Dhruv found himself back at the bin, arm plunging deep into its depths.

His fingers closed around the packet, and relief and self-loathing washed over him. He withdrew his hand, the crumpled packet clutched tightly in his fist. For a moment, he stood there, torn between throwing it back and giving in to his addiction.

With a shaky exhale, Dhruv made his choice.

Dhruv's fingers trembled as he lit the bidi, the familiar smell of tobacco filling the air. He took a deep drag, the smoke burning his lungs, a physical pain that paled in comparison to the emotional turmoil that raged within him.

The smoke curled around him, a hazy veil that seemed to isolate him from the rest of the world. He was alone, trapped in his thoughts, his fears, and his guilt. The weight of his decision was a crushing force, a burden that threatened to consume him.

As the minutes turned into hours, Dhruv sat there, his back against the cold hospital wall, his heart heavy with the knowledge of what he had done. He waited, suspended in this limbo, for the outcome of a decision that would change his life forever.

The sterile hospital corridor faded from Dhruv's consciousness as he slumped against the wall, his mind drifting to happier times. The harsh fluorescent lights dimmed in his vision, replaced by the warm glow of memories. As the weight of his impossible decision pressed down on him, Dhruv found himself seeking refuge in the recollections of his life with Priya.

Their love story unfolded in his mind like a cherished photograph album, each memory a snapshot of joy, growth, and healing.

CHAPTER EIGHT

Unexpected Connections

The harsh fluorescent lights of MedTech's R&D lab buzzed overhead, casting a sterile glow across the workbenches cluttered with circuit boards and half-assembled prototypes. Dhruv hunched over his station, his calloused fingers deftly manipulating a soldering iron as he connected the delicate components of their latest medical sensor. The acrid smell of melting solder filled his nostrils, a scent that had become oddly comforting over the past few months.

He paused, stretching his arms above his head and wincing as his shoulder popped. The long hours bent over intricate electronics were a far cry from the programming work he'd done at TechNova, but Dhruv found a strange solace in the physical nature of his new role. Something was grounding about creating tangible objects, devices that would go on to help people in tangible, measurable ways.

As he rolled his neck, trying to work out the knots that seemed to reside there these days permanently, his gaze drifted to the small mirror affixed to the corner of his workstation. The face that stared back at him was a stark reminder of how much had changed in the past year. The dark circles under his eyes had faded somewhat, no longer the deep purple bruises of constant fear and sleepless nights. His cheekbones were less pronounced, his face filling out as regular meals became the norm rather than the exception.

But it was his eyes that showed the most transformation. Where once there had been a constant wariness, a readiness to flinch at any sudden movement, now there was a cautious hope. The haunted look hadn't disappeared entirely – Dhruv doubted it ever would – but it had receded, making space for something new to grow.

He ran a hand through his hair, longer now than he'd ever been allowed to keep it before. Choosing when to get a haircut felt like a small rebellion, a quiet assertion of control over his body.

"Earth to Dhruv!" A voice cut through his reverie, accompanied by a gentle tap on his shoulder. He turned to see Aisha, one of the senior engineers, grinning at him. "Lost in thought again, huh? Come on, it's time for the team meeting."

Dhruv nodded, carefully setting down his tools and following Aisha to the conference room. As they walked, he marvelled at how easily he moved through the office now, how he no longer flinched when someone called his name or brushed past him in the hallway. The constant state of hypervigilance that had defined so much of his life was slowly, painfully, giving way to something approaching normalcy.

The conference room was already half-full when they arrived, the air thick with the smell of coffee and the low hum of pre-meeting chatter. Dhruv slid into a seat near the back, pulling out his notebook and a pen. He still preferred taking notes by hand, finding that the physical act of writing helped cement information in his mind better than typing ever had.

As the meeting began, Dhruv found his thoughts drifting again, this time to the therapy sessions that had become a fixed part of his monthly routine. Dr. Mehra's gentle guidance had been instrumental in helping him navigate the tumultuous waters of recovery. They had spent countless hours unpacking the years of abuse, examining how Ram's violence had shaped Dhruv's perception of himself and the world around him.

"Recovery isn't linear," Dr. Mehra had reminded him in their last session, her kind eyes holding his gaze steadily. "There will be good days and bad days. The important thing is to keep moving forward, even if it's just a tiny step at a time."

Dhruv had nodded, thinking of the nightmares that still occasionally jolted him awake, drenched in sweat and gasping for air. But those nights were becoming less frequent, the terror less all-consuming. And on the mornings after, he could get up, go to work, and face the day – small victories that would have seemed impossible mere months ago.

A nudge from Aisha brought Dhruv's attention back to the present. Vijay, the project lead, discussed the timeline for their latest prototype. Dhruv quickly jotted down the key points, his mind fully engaged with the task. This was another aspect of his new life that he cherished – the ability to lose himself in work that challenged and fulfilled him without the constant fear of repercussions for any perceived mistake.

Dhruv volunteered to take on an additional project component as the meeting wrapped up. The words left his mouth before he had fully processed them, and for a moment, he felt a flicker of the old panic. But Vijay's approving nod and the encouraging smiles from his teammates washed away the anxiety, replacing it with a warm sense of belonging.

Returning to his workstation, Dhruv pulled up the schematics for the new component on his computer. The complexity of the design was daunting, but he felt a surge of excitement at the challenge. This was why he had chosen to leave the relative safety of his role at TechNova; why he had taken the risk of joining a start-up in a field, he was still learning. Here, he could push himself and grow in ways that went beyond just professional development.

As he immersed himself in the intricate details of the circuit design, Dhruv's mind wandered again, this time to the person who had played such a pivotal role in his journey. Priya's face floated before his mind's eye, her warm smile and encouraging words a balm to his battered spirit even now, months after he had left TechNova.

Their relationship had evolved in ways Dhruv could never have predicted, transitioning from the professional mentorship of boss and employee to something far more personal and profound. He thought back to those early days of the pandemic when the world had shrunk to the confines of their respective apartments, and yet, somehow, their connection had expanded to fill the space between them.

A soft chime from his computer pulled Dhruv back to the present. A new email had arrived, the sender's name causing a flutter in his chest. Priya. Even months into their relationship, seeing her name still brought warmth and excitement. He clicked open the message, a smile spreading as he read her words.

"Dinner tonight? I've got a surprise planned. Don't work too late, genius. ♥? - P"

Dhruv felt a rush of anticipation, tempered with a lingering disbelief that this was his life now. He quickly typed a reply, confirming their plans and adding a heart emoji – another small act, still feeling daringly vulnerable.

As he returned to his work, Dhruv saw his reflection again in the small mirror. The man looking back at him was still a work in progress, still healing, still learning to trust in the goodness of the world and his place in it. But there was a light in his eyes now, a spark of hope and determination that burned brighter with each passing day.

With renewed focus, Dhruv dove back into his project, the gentle whir of cooling fans and the soft clicks of his keyboard creating a soothing backdrop to his thoughts. The past may have left its scars, but the future – his future – was unfolding before him, full of possibilities he was only now beginning to imagine.

As the workday drew close, Dhruv glanced at the clock more frequently, anticipation building for his evening plans with Priya. He carefully packed away his tools, double-checking that everything was in its proper place – a habit born from years of avoiding his father's wrath over any perceived disorder.

The commute home was a blur of familiar sights and sounds: the crowded bus, the bustling streets of Patna gradually giving way to the quieter suburbs. As Dhruv climbed the stairs to his modest apartment, he couldn't help but marvel at how different his life had become in such a short time.

Stepping into his home, he was greeted by the soft glow of the setting sun filtering through the curtains. The space was small but tidy, a far cry from the chaotic environment of his childhood. Dhruv had created a sanctuary for himself, deliberately choosing each piece of furniture and decor.

As he showered and changed for dinner, Dhruv's mind wandered back to the early days of his relationship with Priya, when the world had suddenly shrunk to the size of a computer screen.

It had started innocently enough. With the entire TechNova team working remotely due to the pandemic, Priya instituted daily check-ins with her direct reports. At first, Dhruv had been terrified of these video calls, sure that his inadequacies would be glaringly apparent without the buffer of the office environment. Dhruv dreaded these calls, his anxiety a tight knot in his stomach as Priya's name flashed on his screen day after day.

As the pandemic continued and working from home became a new normal, the routine check-ins became a regular fixture in Priya's week. At first, they had been casual, almost comforting—a way to maintain the team's pulse, even if only through flickering pixels and distorted voices. Her team had always been dependable, their camaraderie natural, and even through the impersonal haze of virtual meetings, they'd shared a few laughs. But as the months stretched on, something began to change.

Now, each check-in felt heavier. The bright chatter from her team was still there, but the energy had shifted. It was as if the screen between them had grown thicker, the distance more than physical. With every new meeting, a quiet dread settled into Priya's chest. She could feel her authority slipping, not because her team was failing but because something intangible was slowly eating away at the connections that once felt effortless.

This meeting was no different. Her team's faces appeared pixelated and faint, a poor substitute for the warmth of real interaction. Her hand tightened around the mug, the warmth barely masking the unease curling tighter in her chest. The metallic tang of instant coffee clung to her tongue as she tried to focus on the meeting.

Her gaze drifted to Dhruv's video feed. He sat, as always, slightly off-centre, his expression carefully neutral as a co-worker recounted a humorous anecdote. But Priya noticed how his fingers tightened around his coffee mug, knuckles bone-white against the chipped ceramic, and how his smile didn't quite reach his eyes - a fleeting shadow of sadness behind the polite facade.

Later, reviewing performance reports, Priya saw the hours Dhruv logged, often stretching into the early hours of the morning. His dedication was undeniable, his skills exceptional, but a knot of worry tightened in her chest. He was brilliant, burning too brightly, like a flame consuming itself from within. She made a mental note to check in with him individually, go beyond the usual work-related conversations, and see if she could do more.

A few weeks later, Priya decided to act on that impulse. "So, Dhruv," Priya had asked one afternoon after they'd discussed his latest project, "what do you do to unwind these days? It can't be all work and no play, even in lockdown."

Dhruv had hesitated, unsure how to respond. The truth was, he didn't know how to 'unwind'. Relaxation had never been a luxury in his father's house.

Sensing his discomfort, Priya continued, "I've been trying to teach myself to cook. It's... not going well." She'd laughed then, a rich, melodious sound that seemed to resonate through the speakers of Dhruv's laptop. "Last night, I nearly set off the smoke alarm to try to make rotis. Can you believe it? I'm twenty-five and can't make a decent roti to save my life."

Her self-deprecating humour had surprised a chuckle out of Dhruv. "I'm not much better," he'd admitted. "I've been living on instant noodles and takeout."

"Oh no, that won't do!" Priya had exclaimed, her eyes twinkling with mischief. "Tell you what, why don't we make it a challenge? We'll try to cook something new this week and compare notes next Friday. The loser has to... hmm... sing a Bollywood song of the winner's choosing on our next call. Deal?"

The prospect should have terrified him. But there was something in Priya's playful smile that made him nod in agreement with how she included him in her world.

That weekend, Dhruv had found himself standing in his tiny kitchen, a laptop propped precariously on the counter as he followed a YouTube tutorial on making dal makhani. The rich aroma of spices had filled his apartment, and for the first time in years, he'd felt a spark of genuine enjoyment in a domestic task.

When Friday rolled around, Dhruv proudly displayed his slightly lumpy but edible dal makhani to the camera. Priya had cheered his success, then sheepishly revealed her creation: a charred mess that was supposedly aloo gobi.

For a stolen moment, as they traded jokes and culinary tips, the weight of work, the pandemic, and the world outside her window faded away. There was just this— the shared laughter, the easy banter, the unexpected spark of connection that transcended the limitations of distance and digital screens. A flicker of doubt, the ever-present voice of caution, whispered in the back of her mind— he was her subordinate, after all. But another part of her dared to hope this was something more.

She reminded herself it was harmless fun, a way to boost morale during a stressful time. Yet, she could not deny a flicker of excitement— a hope that their connection might evolve beyond the professional.

"I think it's safe to say you win this round," she'd laughed, not a trace of bitterness in her defeat. "I hope you're ready for my stunning rendition of 'Chaiyya Chaiyya' next week!"

That had been the turning point. Their weekly cooking challenges became a highlight of Dhruv's otherwise monotonous lockdown life. They branched out into other activities, too: virtual museum tours, online gaming sessions, and even a disastrous attempt at a Zoom dance class that had left them both in stitches.

As the weeks turned into months, Dhruv opened up to Priya in ways he never had with anyone. Late one night, after a particularly gruelling day of remote troubleshooting, he confided in her about his childhood.

"I've never really had a home," he admitted the darkness of his apartment and the lateness of the hour loosening his tongue. "Not a real one, anyway. Home was just... a place to survive."

Priya's face on the screen softened with compassion. "Oh, Dhruv," she'd said softly. "I'm so sorry. No one should have to go through that."

Her simple acknowledgement, free from pity or judgment, had broken something open inside him. Words he'd never dared speak aloud came pouring out: the constant fear, the bruises hidden under long-sleeved shirts, the dreams of escape that had sustained him through the darkest nights.

Priya listened, really listened, in a way no one ever had before. When he finally fell silent, emotionally drained but somehow lighter, she said, "Thank you for trusting me with this, Dhruv. You're powerful, you know that?"

In that moment, seeing himself reflected in Priya's eyes, Dhruv began to believe it might be true.

Priya hung up the phone, but Dhruv's words, raw and laced with pain, continued to echo in the quiet. Sleep, usually a welcome escape, felt impossible now. Images flickered behind her eyelids— the ghostly outline of a belt, the glint of broken glass, the muffled sounds of a child's terror. Her heart ached for the little boy he had been forced to navigate a world shrouded in fear and violence. Yet, amidst the horror, Priya felt a surge of something else. Not pity, but admiration. He had not just endured. He had survived. Escaped. He built a life for himself, brick by fragile brick, on the foundation of a stolen childhood. The sheer strength it took to claw his way out of that darkness filled her with a profound respect. He was more than just a talented engineer. He was a fighter, a survivor, a testament to the indomitable spirit of the human heart. Her heart filled with a newfound tenderness. She vowed to be there for him and offer whatever support she could. Not out of obligation but because she saw and truly saw him and recognised the strength and resilience beneath the surface.

Their relationship deepened, transcending the boundaries of boss and employee and blossoming into a friendship that anchored them both through the uncertainty of the pandemic. Priya shared her own struggles: the weight of familial expectations, her fears of never measuring up, and the loneliness of being a woman in a male-dominated field.

Together, they created a safe space, a virtual haven where they could be vulnerable, silly, and entirely themselves. It was a new experience for Dhruv, this feeling of being truly seen and accepted.

As the world slowly began to open up again, Dhruv found himself both excited and terrified at the prospect of meeting Priya in person. Would the easy rapport they'd developed online translate to the real world? Would she be disappointed when she saw the real him, not just the version framed by a webcam?

His fears had proved unfounded. Their first in-person meeting, in a sun-dappled park with appropriate social distancing, had been awkward and wonderful. Priya's laugh was even more infectious in person, her presence both grounding and exhilarating.

"You know," she'd said, her eyes crinkling with amusement, "I think I like 3D Dhruv even better than 2D Dhruv."

The compliment had made him blush, a warmth spreading through his chest that had nothing to do with the summer heat.

As autumn arrived, bringing with it a gradual easing of restrictions, Dhruv decided to leave TechNova for the opportunity at MedTech. He'd agonised over how to tell Priya, afraid that leaving the company would mean leaving her behind, too.

But Priya had surprised him once again. On his last day at TechNova, after a bittersweet virtual farewell party with the team, she'd asked to speak with him privately.

"Dhruv," she'd said, a hint of nervousness in her voice that he'd never heard before, "I know you're leaving TechNova, but... I was hoping that doesn't mean you're leaving me too. Would you... would you like to go out sometime? Once it's safe, of course."

The question caught him off guard, joy and disbelief warring. "I... yes," he'd managed to stammer out. "I'd like that very much."

Priya's answering smile had been radiant, filling his screen and his heart. "Great," she'd said softly. "It's a date."

As Dhruv adjusted his collar in the mirror, preparing to meet Priya for their dinner date, he marvelled at the journey that had brought him to this point. The man looking back at him from the reflection was far from the scared, broken person he'd been just a year ago.

He was still healing, learning to trust, hope, and love. But with every shared laugh, honest conversation, and a small act of kindness, Priya showed him what it meant to be truly cared for.

As he left his apartment, a spring in his step and anticipation fluttering in his stomach, Dhruv realised that for the first time in his life, he wasn't just surviving. He was beginning to thrive.

The evening air was thick with the scent of jasmine as Dhruv made his way down the bustling street. Patna's nightlife was slowly returning to its pre-pandemic vibrancy, and the sidewalks were alive with the chatter of people eager to reclaim some semblance of normalcy. Dhruv felt excitement and nervousness flutter in his stomach, his palms slightly clammy as he clutched the small bouquet of blue orchids he'd picked up from a street vendor.

He arrived at the restaurant a few minutes early, taking a moment to compose himself before entering. The place was Priya's choice— a small, intimate Goan restaurant in a quiet corner of Kankarbagh. As he stepped inside, the rich aroma of coconut and spices enveloped him.

The interior was warmly lit, with walls adorned with vibrant Azulejo tiles and old sepia-toned photographs of Goa. Soft fado music played in the background, and its melancholic Portuguese lyrics added a touch of wistful romance to the atmosphere. Dhruv felt his nerves settling as the hostess led him to a cosy corner table, partially hidden behind a lush potted palm.

He had just settled into his seat when he saw her. Priya entered the restaurant, and his breath caught in his throat. She was wearing a deep blue salwar kameez that shimmered subtly in the low light, her hair falling in soft waves around her shoulders. As their eyes met, her face lit up with a smile that seemed to outshine every light in the room.

"Hi," she said softly as she approached the table, her voice hinting at the same nervousness Dhruv felt.

"Hi," he replied, standing awkwardly and thrusting the bouquet towards her. "These are for you. I hope you like them."

Priya's eyes sparkled as she accepted the flowers, bringing them to her nose to inhale their spicy-sweet scent. "They're beautiful, Dhruv. Thank you."

As they settled into their seats, Dhruv became hyper-aware of every detail. The soft brush of Priya's knee against his under the small table sent a jolt through him. The candle between them cast a warm glow on her face, highlighting the curve of her cheek and the arch of her brow. He could smell her light, citrusy scent that mingled enticingly with the aromas of the restaurant.

They ordered their meals— fish recheado for Priya, vegetable xacuti for Dhruv— and fell into easy conversation. Despite the nerves and shift in their relationship, talking to Priya felt as natural as breathing.

"So," Priya said, a mischievous glint in her eye as she sipped her solkadhi, "how's life in the exciting world of medical device start-ups? Cured any diseases lately?"

Dhruv laughed, relaxing further into his chair. "Well, I did fix the coffee machine last week. Does that count as a medical breakthrough?"

"Absolutely," Priya nodded solemnly. "Caffeine deficiency is a serious condition. You're practically a hero."

As they bantered, Dhruv marvelled at how far they'd come. The shy, stammering engineer who could barely look his boss in the eye during those video calls seemed like a distant memory. Here, now, he felt seen. Understood. Valued not just for what he could do, but for who he was.

Their food arrived, steam rising from the colourful dishes. Dhruv watched in amusement as Priya's eyes widened at the spiciness of her fish. Without thinking, he offered her a sip of his coconut water, their fingers brushing as she accepted the glass. The simple touch sent a warmth spreading through him that had nothing to do with the spices in his xacuti.

As the evening wore on, their conversation deepened. They spoke of their hopes for the future, fears, and dreams. Priya shared her ambitions to start her own tech company someday, her eyes shining with passion as she outlined her ideas.

Dhruv opened up about his desire to use his skills to make a real difference in people's lives and create devices that could help people.

"You know," Priya said softly, reaching across the table to take his hand, "I always knew you were brilliant. But watching you come into your own these past few months... it's been amazing, Dhruv. You should be proud of how far you've come."

Dhruv felt a lump form in his throat, overwhelmed by the sincerity in her voice. "I couldn't have done it without you," he admitted. "You saw something in me that I couldn't see in myself."

Priya squeezed his hand gently. "I just held up a mirror, Dhruv. The strength was always there inside you."

As they finished their meal, neither seemed eager for the evening to end. They ordered coffee and bebinca for dessert, savouring each bite of the layered pudding as if it could stretch the night out indefinitely.

Finally, as the restaurant began to empty around them, they reluctantly asked for the check. Stepping out into the night air, Dhruv felt a moment of panic. How did he end this? What was the protocol here?

But Priya, as always, seemed to sense his uncertainty. "Walk me home?" she asked, her hand finding his and intertwining their fingers.

They strolled through the quiet streets, the sounds of the city fading to a gentle hum around them. Dhruv was acutely aware of the warmth of Priya's hand in his, the soft sound of her breathing, and how her shoulder occasionally brushed against his arm as they walked.

All too soon, they arrived at her building. They stood facing each other, neither quite ready to say goodnight. Priya looked up at him, her eyes reflecting the streetlights, and Dhruv felt a surge of courage.

He leaned in slowly, giving her plenty of time to pull away if she wanted. Their lips met in a soft, sweet kiss that sent sparks shooting through his entire body. It was brief, chaste even, but Dhruv knew with absolute certainty that his life had irreversibly changed as they parted.

"Goodnight, Dhruv," Priya whispered, her smile radiant.

"Goodnight, Priya," he replied, his voice husky and emotional.

As he walked home, with the cool night air on his face, Dhruv felt like he was floating. The city around him seemed transformed, every sight and sound infused with a new vibrancy. The lingering taste of coconut and spice on his tongue, the phantom pressure of Priya's lips on his, and the memory of her smile combined to create a heady mixture of joy and anticipation for what the future might hold.

For the first time in his life, Dhruv allowed himself to imagine a future filled with love, with companionship, with the kind of understanding and acceptance he'd found with Priya. As he climbed the stairs to his apartment, he realised that the constant knot of tension he'd carried in his chest for as long as he could remember had loosened.

In its place was something new. Something warm and bright and full of promise.

Hope.

CHAPTER NINE

Tender Discoveries

The Patna evening settled over the city like a warm blanket, the last remnants of sunlight painting the sky in hues of orange and pink. In a small apartment nestled in the heart of Rajendra Nagar, Dhruv stood in the kitchen, a look of determination etched on his face. The countertop was a battlefield of ingredients – chopped vegetables, aromatic spices, and pots and pans. He had spent the entire afternoon preparing for this moment, wanting everything to be perfect for Priya.

Priya. The thought of her name sent a flutter through his chest. They had been dating for several months, each day deepening their connection in ways Dhruv had never experienced before. Tonight was to be special – their first truly intimate evening together. The anticipation had been building for weeks, a delicious tension underlying their every interaction.

Dhruv stirred the simmering curry, inhaling deeply. The rich aroma of garam masala and coconut milk filled the air, mingling with the scent of jasmine from the small vase of flowers he had placed on the dining table. Everything had to be perfect.

In the bedroom, Priya stood before the full-length mirror, smoothing down the front of her dress for the hundredth time. It was a deep burgundy, the colour of ripe pomegranates, with delicate gold embroidery along the neckline. She had spent far too long deciding what to wear, wanting to strike the perfect balance between elegant and alluring. Her heart raced with a mixture of excitement and nerves. This wasn't just another date night – they had an unspoken understanding about where the evening might lead.

She closed her eyes, taking a deep breath to centre herself. The faint sounds of Dhruv moving about in the kitchen drifted through the apartment, and a smile tugged at her lips. Just thinking about him – his gentle eyes, warm laugh, and his hand in hers – filled her with a sense of calm and rightness.

Priya opened her eyes and gave herself one last appraising look in the mirror. She reached for her small clutch, fishing out her phone. With a few taps, she pulled up the carefully curated playlist she had spent hours perfecting—romantic Bollywood ballads mixed with soft Western indie tracks – the perfect soundtrack for the evening ahead.

As she made her way towards the living room, the sudden, shrill beep of the smoke alarm pierced the air. Priya's eyes widened in alarm, and she quickened her pace.

"Dhruv?" she called out, worry colouring her voice. "Is everything alright?"

She rounded the corner to find Dhruv frantically waving a kitchen towel at the smoke detector, looking dismayed. The source of the commotion was immediately apparent – a tray of what must have once been garlic bread now resembled charcoal briquettes.

"I'm so sorry!" Dhruv exclaimed, his face flushed with embarrassment. "I got distracted by the curry and completely forgot about the bread!"

Despite the chaos of the moment, Priya couldn't help but laugh. The sight of Dhruv – usually so composed – flailing about with a dish towel was endearingly comical. Her laughter seemed to break the tension, and soon Dhruv joined in, the absurdity of the situation hitting them both.

As the alarm finally fell silent, they stood there, breathless from laughter, gazing at each other. Dhruv's eyes roamed over Priya, taking in the sight of her. "You look... stunning," he said softly, his voice filled with awe.

Priya felt a blush creep up her cheeks under his admiring gaze. "Thank you," she replied, equally soft. "You're not looking too bad yourself, Chef Dhruv – even with a bit of smoke clinging to you."

Dhruv groaned. "Some chef I turned out to be. I wanted everything to be perfect, and instead, I burnt the garlic bread into charcoal."

Priya stepped closer, reaching out to straighten his slightly askew collar. "Hey," she said gently, her fingers lingering on his chest. "It's already perfect because we're together. Besides," she added with a mischievous glint, "I've always preferred my garlic bread on the... well-done side."

Dhruv's laughter rumbled through his chest, and Priya felt it beneath her fingertips. The moment stretched between them, charged with an electric undercurrent of attraction and anticipation.

Clearing his throat, Dhruv reluctantly stepped back. "Well, burnt offering aside, dinner is just about ready. Why don't you get comfortable while I plate everything up?"

Priya nodded, moving towards the small dining area. Dhruv had transformed the space, draping a crisp white tablecloth over the usually bare table. A slender vase holding three perfect red roses served as a centrepiece, flanked by tall, unlit candles. The effort he had put into creating a romantic atmosphere touched her deeply.

As she settled into her chair, Priya remembered her playlist. "Oh! I almost forgot," she said, pulling out her phone. "I made us some mood music."

She tapped the screen, frowning when nothing happened. Another tap. Still silence. "Come on," she muttered, growing frustrated as she navigated through the settings.

Dhruv emerged from the kitchen, carefully balancing two steaming plates. "Everything okay?" he asked, noting her furrowed brow.

Priya sighed in exasperation. "The stupid phone won't connect to your speakers. I spent ages on this playlist, and now it won't even play!"

Setting down the plates, Dhruv moved behind her chair, peering over her shoulder at the phone. "Here, let me try," he offered. Their heads bent close together as they fiddled with the device, a comfortable intimacy in their proximity.

After several failed attempts and increasingly creative curses from Priya, they admitted defeat. "You know what?" Dhruv said, straightening up. "We don't need music. The only sound I want to hear tonight is your voice."

The sincerity in his words made Priya's heart skip a beat. She looked up at him, struck once again by how handsome he was – not in a conventional movie-star way, but in a manner uniquely his own. His warm brown eyes crinkled at the corners when he smiled; right now, that smile was directed solely at her.

"Smooth talker," she teased, but the warmth in her voice belied her words.

Dhruv's grin widened as he moved to light the candles. The soft, flickering light cast a warm glow over the table, softening the edges of the room and creating an intimate atmosphere.

As they began to eat, the initial nervousness that had coloured the beginning of the evening began to fade. Conversation flowed easily between them, punctuated by comfortable silences and shared laughter. Priya raved about the curry, causing Dhruv to beam with pride.

"I'm glad at least one dish turned out well," he said, gesturing towards the conspicuously empty bread basket.

Priya reached across the table, intertwining her fingers with his. "Everything is wonderful, Dhruv. Truly."

The weight of the moment settled over them, heavy with promise and unspoken desires. Dhruv's thumb traced small circles on the back of Priya's hand, sending shivers up her arm.

"Should we move to the couch?" Dhruv suggested, his voice low and slightly husky.

Priya nodded, not trusting herself to speak. They cleared the table together, hands brushing against each other more often than strictly necessary, each touch igniting sparks beneath their skin.

As they settled onto the couch, the narrow space brought them closer together. Priya tucked her legs beneath her, angling her body towards Dhruv. The candlelight played across his features, highlighting the strong line of his jaw and the fullness of his lips.

Dhruv reached out, tucking a stray strand of hair behind Priya's ear. His hand lingered, cupping her cheek gently. "You are so beautiful," he murmured, his eyes roaming her face as if memorising every detail.

Priya leaned into his touch, her heart pounding so loudly she was sure he must be able to hear it. "Dhruv," she whispered, her voice barely audible.

It was unclear who moved first, but their lips met in a kiss that stole the breath from their lungs. Unlike their previous kisses – sweet, exploratory things – this one was filled with hunger and need. Priya's hands found their way to Dhruv's hair, her fingers tangling in the soft curls at the nape of his neck.

Dhruv's arms encircled her waist, drawing her closer until she was practically in his lap. His lips left hers to trail kisses along her jaw and throat. Priya tilted her head back, a soft gasp escaping her as he found a particularly sensitive spot below her ear.

"Is this okay?" Dhruv murmured against her skin, ever considerate even in the heat of the moment.

"More than okay," Priya breathed, guiding his lips back to hers.

As their kisses grew more heated, hands began to roam increasingly boldly. Priya's fingers worked at the buttons of Dhruv's shirt while his hands skimmed the curves of her waist and hips.

When they finally broke apart, both were breathing heavily. Dhruv rested his forehead against Priya's, their breaths mingling in the scant space between them.

"Maybe we should move this to the bedroom?" Priya suggested her voice low and filled with want.

Dhruv nodded, pressing one more quick kiss to her lips before standing. He offered his hand to Priya, helping her up from the couch. They went to the bedroom, pausing every few steps to exchange heated kisses.

Once in the bedroom, illuminated only by the soft glow of the bedside lamp, a sudden shyness seemed to overtake them both. They stood at the foot of the bed, the enormity of the moment weighing heavily in the air.

Priya reached for the zipper of her dress, but her usually nimble fingers fumbled with the clasp. Dhruv stepped behind her, gently brushing her hands away. "Let me," he said softly.

With infinite care, he lowered the zipper, his knuckles grazing the smooth skin of her back. Priya shivered at his touch, goosebumps rising in her arms despite the warmth of the room.

As the dress pooled at her feet, Priya turned to face Dhruv. His eyes roamed her body with awe and desire, making her feel powerful and vulnerable. She reached for him, her hands sliding beneath his open shirt to push it off his shoulders.

Clad now only in their undergarments, they came together in another kiss. This one was slower, deeper, and filled with promise and exploration. Dhruv's hands spanned Priya's waist, lifting her slightly as he lowered her onto the bed.

A bubble of nervous laughter escaped her as Priya's back hit the cool sheets. Dhruv pulled back slightly, a question in his eyes.

"Sorry," Priya giggled, covering her face with her hands. "I just... I've been imagining this moment for so long, and now that it's here, I feel like a fumbling teenager again."

Dhruv's face softened with understanding and affection. He gently pried her hands away from her face, kissing each palm. "We can take this as slow as you want," he assured her. "There's no rush."

Priya's heart swelled with love for this man who always put her comfort first. She reached up, tracing the line of his jaw with her fingertips. "I love you," she said softly, the words slipping out before she could even think to stop them.

For a moment, Dhruv froze, his eyes wide with surprise. Then, a smile bloomed across his face, radiant and joy-filled. "I love you too," he replied, his voice thick with emotion. "So much."

Their next kiss was tender and unhurried, a physical manifestation of the words they had just shared. As they continued to explore each other, hands roaming and lips tasting, the last barriers between them fell away.

Priya's fingers trailed down Dhruv's back, mapping the planes of his muscles. Suddenly, she felt it – a change in texture beneath her fingertips. Her hands stilled as she realised what she was feeling.

In the soft light of the bedside lamp, she saw them clearly for the first time – a network of scars crisscrossing Dhruv's back and torso. Some were faint, barely visible lines of silvery white. Others were more prominent, raised welts that spoke of deeper wounds.

"Dhruv," she whispered, her voice catching in her throat.

Dhruv tensed above her, suddenly vulnerable in a way that had nothing to do with his nudity. "I... I should have warned you," he stammered, reaching for the discarded sheet to cover himself.

Priya caught his hand, stopping him. "No," she said softly, her eyes meeting his. "Please... can I?"

Dhruv searched her face for a long moment before nodding, not trusting his voice. Gently, Priya guided him to lie on his stomach, giving her full access to his back.

She explored the map of scars etched across his skin with infinite tenderness. Her touch was feather-light, almost reverent, as she traced each mark. "This one?" she asked softly, her fingers ghosting over a thin scar below his left shoulder blade.

Dhruv swallowed hard, his voice barely above a whisper. "I was seven. Broke a plate while doing dishes."

Priya leaned down, pressing her lips to the scar in a gentle kiss. Dhruv shivered beneath her, not from cold but from the tenderness of the gesture.

Her fingers moved to a longer scar that curved around his ribs. "Eleven," Dhruv said unprompted, his voice hollow with remembered pain. "Came home late from school."

Another kiss, soft and healing, was placed on this scar.

Priya's hand drifted lower, finding a cluster of small, round scars near his hip. Her breath caught as she realised what they must be. "Cigarette burns," Dhruv confirmed, his voice detached as if speaking about someone else's body. "I don't remember why."

Priya's lips lingered here as if trying to kiss away years of pain and trauma. She felt a lump forming in her throat, her heart aching for the boy Dhruv had been, for all he had endured.

Slowly, reverently, she continued to map each scar. Some had stories attached – a fall from a tree, a cooking accident. Others, Dhruv, couldn't remember the specific incidents that caused them. It didn't matter. With each touch, each kiss, Priya wordlessly told him: You are not these scars. You are not your pain. You are loved.

A particularly jagged scar ran across his lower back. As Priya's fingers brushed it, Dhruv flinched involuntarily. She immediately withdrew her hand, not wanting to cause him any discomfort.

"This one?" she asked gently, giving him the space to share or not as he chose.

Dhruv was quiet for so long that Priya thought he might not answer. When he finally spoke, his voice was raw with emotion. "The night I left," he said, the words seeming to cost him greatly. "I was sixteen. He... my father... he'd been drinking more than usual." He paused, lost in the memory. "The belt broke. The buckle..."

He trailed off, but Priya understood. Tears welled in her eyes, spilling silently down her cheeks. She wrapped her arms around him from behind, pressing her cheek between his shoulder blades. Dhruv felt the wetness of her tears against his skin.

"I'm so sorry," she whispered, her voice choked with emotion.

Dhruv turned in her embrace, cupping her face in his hands. His thumbs gently wiped away her tears. "Don't be," he said, his voice stronger now. "You're healing me, Priya. In ways I never thought possible."

Their eyes met, a world of understanding passing between them. In that moment, something shifted – a deepening of their connection, a breaking down of the last walls between them.

Their lovemaking that night was slow and tender, rewriting all the ways touch had been used to hurt. With each caress and kiss, they built something new, something healing, something holy.

CHAPTER TEN

Broken Glasses

But as the initial wave of nostalgia ebbed, Dhruv became acutely aware of his surroundings again. The hard linoleum floor beneath him, the distant beeping of medical equipment, the hushed voices of nurses passing by— it all anchored him firmly in the present.

He glanced at the clock on the wall, its hands moving with agonising slowness. How long had he been sitting here? Minutes? Hours? Time had lost all meaning in this liminal space of waiting and worrying.

Dhruv's gaze fell to his hands, noticing for the first time how they trembled slightly. He clenched them into fists, trying to still the tremor, but it persisted— a physical manifestation of the turmoil within him.

A nurse walked by, her shoes squeaking softly on the polished floor. Dhruv looked up, hope flaring briefly in his chest, but she continued without glancing. Not news about Priya, then. The hope faded as quickly as it had come, leaving behind a hollow ache.

He leaned his head back against the wall, closing his eyes. His decision echoed in his mind— "Save Priya." Had he made the right choice? The guilt of potentially sacrificing their unborn child weighed heavily on him, a burden that threatened to crush his spirit.

As he sat there, trapped in this purgatory of his own making, Dhruv found his thoughts drifting again to Priya. But this time, instead of their early days together, his mind settled on a memory from later in their relationship. A memory that encapsulated the healing and growth they had fostered in each other.

It was an ordinary evening, unremarkable in its domesticity, yet it held a profound significance in Dhruv's healing journey.

The small bathroom in their first apartment materialised in his mind's eye. Steam curled around Priya as she stood at the sink, her hair piled messily atop her head, brushing her teeth. Dhruv leaned against the doorframe, admiring the curve of her spine and how her oversized t-shirt slipped off one shoulder. The intimacy of the moment, the sheer ordinariness of it, filled him with a warmth he had never known in his childhood home.

A mischievous grin spread across his face. He tiptoed to the sink, cupped his hands under the running tap, and flicked a spray of cool water at Priya's exposed shoulder.

She yelped, toothbrush clattering into the sink. "Dhruv!" she sputtered, laughing as she wiped toothpaste from her chin. "Oh, you're in for it now."

Before he could react, she'd scooped water from the tap, thoroughly soaking his shirt. Dhruv lunged playfully for the tap, and soon, they were both drenched, giggling like children in the confined space. The laughter echoed off the tiled walls, a joyous sound that seemed to chase away the shadows of his past.

"Well," Priya said, peeling off her wet shirt, "might as well have a proper shower now."

They squeezed into the narrow corner where the showerhead hung, the space intimate in its constraints.

Soap-slick hands explored familiar curves, playful touches interspersed with tender kisses. Dhruv marvelled at how something as simple as bathing could feel so joyous, so safe. It was a far cry from his childhood home's tense, fearful atmosphere, where even the most mundane activities could trigger his father's volatile temper.

As Priya turned to rinse her hair, Dhruv's elbow knocked against the glass corner shelf. Time seemed to slow as he watched it teeter, then crash to the tiled floor, shattering into a glittering spray of shards.

The sound of breaking glass echoed in his ears, transforming into a memory he'd long tried to forget. The warm, safe cocoon of the present dissolved, replaced by his past's cold, harsh reality.

Six-year-old Dhruv stood frozen, staring at the broken glass at his feet. He'd only wanted a drink of water. But the glass had been slippery, and now...

The heavy tread of his father's footsteps made Dhruv's heart race. "What did you do, you clumsy fool?" Ram's voice boomed, filling the small kitchen. The words seemed to reverberate through time, shaking Dhruv to his core.

"I'm sorry, Baba," Dhruv whispered, his voice trembling. "It was an accident. I'll clean it up."

But Ram was already reaching for his belt, the buckle jangling ominously. "I'll teach you to be careful," he growled, his eyes dark with anger and the influence of alcohol.

Dhruv closed his eyes, bracing for the familiar sting of leather against his skin. He could almost feel the bite of the belt and hear the whistle as it cut through the air. His muscles tensed, a learned response to the impending pain.

"Dhruv? Dhruv, love, look at me."

Priya's gentle voice cut through the memory like a lifeline. Dhruv blinked, realising he was pressed against the damp bathroom wall, arms instinctively shielding his head. The warm water still pattered against his back from the showerhead above, grounding him in the present.

Priya stood perfectly still, her eyes full of understanding. She didn't try to touch him, intuitively knowing he needed space in the confined area. Her presence was a stark contrast to his father's looming, threatening figure in his memory.

"It's okay," she said softly. "It was an accident. No one is angry."

Dhruv lowered his arms slowly, his breathing ragged. He looked at Priya, really looking at her, seeing the love and concern in her eyes. It was so different from the fear and anger he was used to seeing in moments like these.

"I... I broke your shelf," he stammered, the words feeling inadequate. "I'm so sorry. I'll replace it, I'll clean it up, I—"

"Shh," Priya soothed, her voice a gentle caress. "It's just a shelf. Are you hurt? Did you cut yourself?"

The concern in her voice, so at odds with his memory, made Dhruv's throat tight. He shook his head, unable to speak. The kindness in her words was almost too much to bear, a balm he didn't know how to accept.

"Good," Priya smiled, relief evident in her expression. "That's all that matters. We'll clean it up together after we shower, okay?"

She held out her hand, a silent invitation. Dhruv hesitated momentarily, the echoes of his past still ringing in his ears. Then, slowly, he reached out and took her hand, allowing her to pull him back under the warm spray gently.

As she began to hum softly, washing his hair with tender care in the small space they shared, Dhruv felt the tension slowly leave his body. The familiar scent of her shampoo mingled with the steam, creating a cocoon of comfort around him. Her fingers massaged his scalp, each touch an affirmation of love and acceptance.

Here, in this tiny bathroom with broken glass on the floor and love filling every corner, another shard of his past began to heal. The contrast between this moment and his childhood memories was stark. Where there had been pain, there was now gentleness. Where there had been fear, there was now safety.

Dhruv closed his eyes, letting the warm water wash over him, imagining it carrying away the remnants of his painful past. He focused on the sensation of Priya's hands in his hair, the sound of her soft humming, and the warmth of her body close to his. He realised this was what it meant to be truly safe, truly loved.

As they finished their shower, Priya wrapped Dhruv in a fluffy towel, her movements slow and deliberate. She didn't push him to talk, didn't demand explanations. Instead, she existed with him in the moment, her presence a silent support.

Later, as they carefully swept up the glass together, Dhruv paused, looking at Priya with eyes full of wonder and gratitude. The simple act of cleaning up together, without anger or recrimination, felt profoundly healing.

"Thank you," he said softly, his voice thick with emotion.

Priya tilted her head, a questioning look on her face. "For what?"

"For showing me that accidents don't have to end in pain. For... for loving me through the broken pieces."

Priya set down the dustpan, taking Dhruv's hands in hers. Her touch was gentle, her palms warm against his skin. "That's what love is, Dhruv," she said, her eyes shining with affection. "It's not about perfection. It's about holding each other through the messy, broken moments. And building something beautiful from them."

Dhruv pulled her close, breathing in the clean scent of her damp hair. At that moment, he made a silent promise to himself and Priya. To keep learning, keep healing, keep loving – even when it meant facing the shattered pieces of his past.

As they finished cleaning, Dhruv felt a shift within himself. The memory of the broken glass, once a trigger for fear and pain, had been transformed. It was now a testament to the healing power of love, a reminder that he was no longer that frightened little boy, helpless in the face of his father's rage.

That night, as they lay in bed, Dhruv opened up to Priya about his childhood in a way he never had before. The words came haltingly at first, then in a rush, as if a dam had broken. He told her about the constant fear and the unpredictability of his father's moods.

Priya listened without judgment, her hand a steady presence in his. When he faltered, she squeezed his fingers gently, encouraging him to continue. And when the tears came, she held him close, her own eyes glistening with empathy.

Priya's heart ached for him, for the weight of that fear, the burden of a past that refused to be ignored. But even as he voiced his deepest terror, Priya saw the very thing that set him apart from the man who had inflicted so much pain. It was there in the tremor of his voice, in his fierce grip on her hand, in the depths of his eyes, a silent plea for reassurance, a desperate desire to break free from the cycle that had haunted him for so long.

"You're so strong, Dhruv," she whispered as he finished speaking. "Look at how far you've come. You've broken the cycle. You're not your father, and you never will be."

Her words were a balm to his soul, soothing fears he'd carried for so long. Dhruv realised that in sharing his pain with Priya, he'd taken another step towards healing. The burden he'd carried for so long felt lighter, shared between them.

As they drifted off to sleep, Dhruv felt a sense of peace he'd rarely known. While not wholly exorcised, the ghosts of his past seemed less threatening. With Priya by his side, he felt capable of facing anything.

The memory faded, leaving Dhruv again aware of his surroundings in the hospital corridor. The stark contrast between the warmth of that recollection and the cold reality of his current situation hit him like a physical blow.

He thought about the journey he and Priya had taken together and the healing they had fostered in each other. She had shown him what it meant to be loved unconditionally and accepted despite his flaws and past. She had taught him that vulnerability wasn't weakness but strength.

And now, faced with an impossible choice, he had chosen her. The guilt of potentially sacrificing their unborn child weighed heavily on him, but beneath it was an unshakeable certainty. Priya was his anchor, his safe harbour. Without her, he feared he would be lost, adrift in a sea of his trauma and fear.

Dhruv closed his eyes, tears slipping down his cheeks. He prayed to whatever higher power might be listening, begging Priya and their child to survive. But if only one could be saved, he knew it had to be Priya.

Dhruv made another silent vow as he sat back against the cold hospital wall. If Priya survived this, he would dedicate every day to being worthy of her love. He would face his fears, confront his past, and strive to be the man she believed he could be. And if their child survived too, he would be the father he had never had – loving, supportive, and kind.

The minutes ticked by, each one feeling like an eternity. Dhruv remained there, trapped in limbo, waiting for news that would change his life forever. But even in this moment of uncertainty and fear, he held onto the warmth of his memories with Priya. They were a reminder of the strength they had found in each other, a beacon of hope in the darkness of this long night.

As dawn began to break, painting the hospital corridor in soft hues of pink and gold, Dhruv's mind slowly returned to the present. The memory of that night with Priya, the broken shelf and the healing that followed had been a balm to his troubled soul.

He blinked, his eyes adjusting to the changing light. The hospital was beginning to stir with the activity of shift changes and early morning routines. A fresh-faced nurse walked by, offering Dhruv a sympathetic smile.

Dhruv felt a renewed sense of strength despite the long night of waiting, despite the weight of his decision and the uncertainty that still hung in the air. The memory had reminded him of the journey he and Priya had taken together, of the love and healing they had found in each other.

Whatever news the coming hours might bring, Dhruv knew he would face it with the resilience that Priya had helped him discover within himself. He straightened his back, ready to meet whatever challenges lay ahead.

As fear and anticipation coursed through him, Dhruv held onto the warmth of his memories with Priya. They were a reminder of the strength they had found in each other, a beacon of hope in the darkness of this long night.

With a deep breath, Dhruv stepped forward to meet the doctor, ready to face whatever the future held. The journey ahead would not be easy, but with the memory of Priya's love to guide him, he felt prepared to take it on, one step at a time.

CHAPTER ELEVEN

Echoes of Her Heartbeat

The sharp, sterile scent of the hospital clamped around Dhruv's throat, choking him. He paced back and forth, his footsteps echoing off the sterile white walls. The fluorescent lights buzzed overhead, their harsh glow making the world feel unreal as if he were trapped in some bizarre dream. But this was no dream. This was the day his life would change forever, though not in the way he had imagined.

Dhruv's mind wandered back to the morning, replaying the events that had led them here. Priya's excited voice, tinged with a hint of nervousness, as she shook him awake. "It's time," she had said, her eyes wide with anticipation. The rush to the hospital, the breathless check-in at the maternity ward, the reassuring smiles of the nurses as they wheeled Priya away. It had all seemed so routine, so normal.

Now, hours later, the air felt thick with tension. Dhruv's shirt clung to his back, damp with nervous sweat. He ran a hand through his dishevelled hair, trying to calm the storm of thoughts in his mind. Why was it taking so long? Was everything okay?

A nurse rushed past, the sway of her uniform jolting Dhruv back to the present. He opened his mouth to ask for an update but closed it again as she disappeared around a corner. The waiting was unbearable.

Dhruv leaned against the wall, closing his eyes. He thought of Priya, her strength, her unwavering optimism. She had been his rock through so much – his escape from his father's abuse, his struggles to build a new life, his journey of healing. Now, it was his turn to be strong for her, for their child.

The memory of their last conversation before she was taken into the delivery room flooded his mind. Priya's face was flushed with exertion and excitement, her hand gripping his tightly. "We're going to be parents, Dhruv," she had said, her voice filled with wonder. "Can you believe it?"

He had kissed her forehead, overwhelmed by love and gratitude. "You're going to be an amazing mother," he had told her. The faith in her eyes had been absolute, chasing away his doubts and fears.

As the minutes ticked by with agonising slowness, those fears crept back in. Dhruv's mind conjured worst-case scenarios, each more terrifying than the last. He tried to push them away, focusing instead on the future they had planned. They painted the nursery together, and the soft yellow walls were adorned with cartoon animals. The tiny clothes folded neatly in drawers, waiting for their owner. The list of names they had agonised over, finally settling on one that felt perfect.

A commotion down the hall caught Dhruv's attention. He straightened up, heart pounding, as he saw a group of medical staff rushing towards the delivery room. The world seemed to slow down, each second stretching into eternity as he waited for news.

The delivery room door opened, and a different cry filled the air – a newborn's wail. The sound pierced through the haze of Dhruv's anxiety, igniting a spark of joy in his chest. He took a step forward, a smile forming on his lips.

But as quickly as it had come, the joy evaporated. The doctor emerged, his face etched with lines of fatigue and something else – something that made Dhruv's blood run cold. The world narrowed to a pinpoint. All sound faded away except for the thundering of his heartbeat.

"Mr Sharma," the doctor began, his voice gentle but heavy with the weight of what he was about to say. "This is tough news to share, and I know it's a lot to take in, but I'm afraid I have some bad news for you."

Dhruv felt the floor tilt beneath his feet. He gripped the wall for support, struggling to process the words. "Bad news?" he repeated, his voice sounding distant and unfamiliar to his ears. "Is Priya okay? Is our baby alright?"

The doctor placed a comforting hand on Dhruv's shoulder. "Your daughter is healthy," he said, and relief washed over Dhruv for a moment. But the doctor's expression remained grim. "However, our wife experienced severe postpartum haemorrhaging. We've been doing everything we can for her, but..."

The words faded into a dull roar as understanding dawned on Dhruv. This couldn't be happening. Not to Priya. Not to them. They had overcome so much and survived so much. This was supposed to be their happily ever after.

"No," Dhruv whispered, shaking his head. "No, there must be something else you can do. Please, you have to save her."

The doctor's eyes were filled with compassion and regret. "I'm so sorry, Mr Sharma. We've exhausted all options. The bleeding... it's just too severe. Your wife is asking for you. I think... I think it's time to say goodbye."

The world fell away. Dhruv felt as if he were falling, tumbling through an endless void. This wasn't real. It couldn't be real. Any moment now, he would wake up, and Priya would be there, smiling, telling him it was just a bad dream.

But the cold fluorescent lights, the antiseptic smell, the sorrowful eyes of the doctor – it was all too vivid, too painful to be anything but reality. Dhruv's legs moved of their own accord, carrying him into the delivery room, each step feeling like a mile.

The delivery room was a flurry of activity, with medical staff moving urgently. But for Dhruv, time seemed to stand still as his eyes found Priya. She lay on the bed, her skin pale and clammy, her chest rising and falling with shallow breaths. Despite the chaos around her, her eyes were clear and focused, searching the room until they locked onto Dhruv's.

"Dhruv," she whispered, her voice barely audible over the beeping of machines. He was at her side instantly, taking her hand in his and bringing it to his lips.

"I'm here, my love," he said, fighting to keep his voice steady. "I'm right here."

Priya's lips curved into a weak smile. "Our daughter," she said. "Is she...?"

"She's perfect," Dhruv assured her, tears blurring his vision. "Just like her mother."

A nurse approached, cradling a small bundle. With infinite gentleness, she placed the newborn in Priya's arms. Dhruv watched as Priya's face transformed, love and wonder chasing away the pain briefly.

"Hello, little one," Priya murmured, her finger tracing the baby's cheek. "You're so beautiful." She looked up at Dhruv, her eyes shining. "What should we name her?"

Dhruv's heart clenched. They had discussed names for months, but he felt lost when faced with the reality that Priya might not be there to call their daughter by name. "What do you think?" he asked, his voice cracking.

Priya's gaze returned to the baby, a soft smile on her lips. "Priya," she whispered. "A part of me that will always be with you."

Dhruv nodded, unable to speak past the lump in his throat. He leaned down, pressing his forehead to Priya's, their tears mingling. For a moment, they were suspended in time – a family, whole and complete.

But the moment couldn't last. Priya's breathing became more laboured, and her grip on Dhruv's hand weakened. The medical staff moved in, gently taking the baby, their voices a blur of medical jargon that Dhruv couldn't begin to comprehend.

"Dhruv," Priya said, her voice fading. "Promise me... promise me you'll be happy. That you'll live for both of us."

"I can't," Dhruv choked out. "I can't without you. Please, Priya, don't leave me."

Priya's eyes, filled with love and sorrow, met his. "You can," she whispered. "You're the strongest person I know. Our daughter needs you. Live for her, for the life we dreamed of."

Dhruv nodded, unable to deny her this last request. He leaned in, pressing his lips to hers in a final, desperate kiss. "I love you," he breathed against her skin. "I'll always love you."

Priya's lips curved into a smile. "I love you too," she murmured. "Always."

And then, with a soft sigh, Priya's eyes fluttered closed. The steady beep of the heart monitor flattened into a continuous tone, a sound that would haunt Dhruv's nightmares for years to come.

The world shattered around him, fragmenting into a million pieces of grief and disbelief. Dhruv collapsed onto Priya's still form, his body wracked with sobs, as the medical staff moved around him in a blur of motion and muffled voices.

At that moment, as the love of his life slipped away, Dhruv felt as if a part of his soul had been torn away. The future they had planned, the life they were supposed to share – it all crumbled to dust, leaving behind an abyss of loss and pain that seemed impossible to bridge.

The next few hours passed in a haze of grief and confusion. Dhruv felt as if he were watching events unfold from a great distance, disconnected from his own body and the world around him. Doctors and nurses came and went, their voices a meaningless buzz in his ears. Forms were thrust before him, requiring signatures he couldn't remember giving. Through it all, a single thought echoed in his mind: Priya is gone. Priya is gone. Priya is gone.

At some point – minutes or hours later, Dhruv couldn't tell – he found himself in a small, private room. The harsh fluorescent lights had been dimmed, casting soft shadows on the walls. In his arms was a bundle, warm and impossibly small. Priya, his daughter, the last gift Priya had given him.

Dhruv stared down at the sleeping infant, trying to reconcile the joy of her arrival with the devastating loss of his wife. Priya's tiny hand curled around his finger, an anchor in the storm of his grief. She had Priya's nose, he realised with a start, and the same delicate curve of her eyebrows. The observation sent a fresh wave of pain through him, so intense he could barely breathe.

"I'm sorry," he whispered to the baby, his voice hoarse from crying. "I'm so sorry you'll never know her. She would have loved you so much."

Priya stirred in her sleep, her face scrunching up before relaxing again. Dhruv marvelled at her peacefulness and innocence. She had no idea of the tragedy that had marked her entry into the world, no concept of the loss she had suffered before she could even comprehend it.

A soft knock at the door pulled Dhruv from his reverie. He looked to see a nurse enter, her face etched with sympathy. "Mr. Sharma," she said gently, "your in-laws have arrived. Would you like to see them?"

Dhruv's heart clenched. Priya's parents. How could he face them? How could he tell them that their daughter was gone? But he nodded, steeling himself for what was to come.

Moments later, Mr. and Mrs. Roy entered the room. Their faces were pale, etched with shock and sorrow. Mrs. Sharma's eyes were red-rimmed, tears flowing freely down her cheeks. Mr. Sharma stood rigidly, his jaw clenched as if holding back a scream.

For a long moment, no one spoke. The air was thick with grief, with unspoken accusations and shared pain. Finally, Mrs. Roy broke the silence with a choked sob, collapsing into a nearby chair.

"I'm so sorry," Dhruv choked out, the words feeling hollow and inadequate. "I... I don't know what to say."

Mr. Roy turned to him, his eyes hard with barely contained anguish and anger. "You should have insisted on a C-section," he said, his voice low and accusing. "If you had—"

"Please," Mrs. Roy interrupted, her voice wavering. "Not now. Not here."

The tension in the room was palpable, grief manifesting as anger, confusion, and guilt. Dhruv felt the weight of Mr. Roy's words like a physical blow. Had he failed Priya? Should he have pushed harder for different treatment? The thoughts swirled in his mind, threatening to pull him under.

As if sensing the turmoil, Priya began to fuss in Dhruv's arms. The sound seemed to break through the fog of grief that had settled over the room. Mrs. Roy looked up, focusing on the baby for the first time.

"Is that...?" she asked, her voice barely above a whisper.

Dhruv nodded, carefully standing and moving towards his mother-in-law. "This is Priya," he said softly. "It's... it's what Priya wanted to name her."

Mrs. Roy reached out with trembling hands, and Dhruv gently placed the baby in her arms. As she gazed down at her granddaughter, Fresh tears spilled from her eyes, but these were different, mingled with bittersweet joy.

"She looks just like Priya did," Mrs. Roy murmured, her finger tracing the baby's cheek. "Oh, my sweet girl..."

Even Mr. Roy's hard expression softened as he looked at his granddaughter. He placed a hand on his wife's shoulder, leaning in to get a better look at the baby. For a moment, the room was quiet save for Priya's soft coos.

A nurse gently suggested that Dhruv and the grandparents take turns holding her, which was a tangible reminder of Priya's enduring love. As they passed the baby between them, a fragile bond began to form – three broken hearts united by their love for the woman they had lost and the child who now carried her name.

CHAPTER TWELVE

The Descent

Hours blurred into days, days into weeks. Grief had become Dhruv's atmosphere, a thick, suffocating fog that clung to him, making each breath a labour. The world continued to turn, oblivious to the gaping hole in his heart, and he resented it for its indifference.

Priya grew, and each milestone was a bittersweet reminder of what Priya was missing. Her first smile, her first laugh, her first hiccup – each moment was a celebration tinged with grief. Dhruv documented everything meticulously, talking to Priya as if she could hear him and telling her about their daughter's progress.

"She has your laugh," he would say to the empty room, his voice cracking. "God, Priya, I wish you could see her."

The Roys were a constant presence, their grief mingling with fierce protectiveness over their granddaughter. They helped where they could, but there was an undercurrent of tension that never entirely dissipated. Mr. Roy's words from the hospital lingered, unspoken but ever-present.

Dhruv threw himself into fatherhood with a desperate intensity, determined to be everything his daughter needed. But in the quiet moments, when the baby was asleep and the house fell silent, the pain would overwhelm him. He would find himself curled up on the floor of what should have been their shared bedroom, clutching one of Priya's sweaters to his chest, breathing in her fading scent.

Work became both a refuge and a torment. Colleagues walked on eggshells around him, their pitying glances and awkward condolences only highlighting the enormity of his loss.

One evening, after a challenging day filled with memories and what-ifs, Dhruv stood before the liquor store. He hadn't had a drink since before Priya's pregnancy, their decision to abstain in solidarity. Now, the promise of numbness called to him like a siren song.

"Just one," he told himself as he purchased a bottle of whiskey. "Just to take the edge off."

But one drink turned into two, then three, then the entire bottle. As the alcohol coursed through his system, memories of his father, Ram, flashed through his mind. The stink of cheap liquor on his breath, the sound of his belt whistling through the air, the pain of impact. Dhruv had sworn he would never be like that or touch a drop.

"I'm sorry," he slurred, unsure if he was apologising to Priya, little Priya, or his younger self. "I'm so sorry."

The following day, Dhruv woke to the sound of Priya's cries. He stumbled to his feet, his head pounding, his mouth dry. The memory of the night before flooded back, bringing with it a wave of shame and guilt. He had broken his promise to Priya on more than one occasion. He had succumbed to the darkness he had fought so hard to escape.

He found Priya in her crib, her face flushed with tears. He scooped her up, his arms trembling with the effort, and held her close. "Shhh, it's okay," he whispered, his voice thick with remorse and guilt. "Daddy's here."

He tried to ignore the throbbing ache in his head, the taste of bile in his throat. He had to be strong for her, for

Priya. He had to be better.

But the urge for another drink, the promise of oblivion, was a relentless shadow lurking at the edge of his thoughts. He fought it off, telling himself it was a temporary weakness, a momentary lapse. He lifted his daughter, her innocent eyes meeting his bloodshot ones, and felt a wave of self-loathing.

"I'm sorry, baby," he whispered, rocking her gently. "Daddy made a mistake. It won't happen again."

But it did happen again. And again. The bottle became a crutch, a way to numb the pain that threatened to consume him. Dhruv told himself he could control it, that he wasn't like his father. But the lines began to blur, and his promises to himself in the harsh light of day crumbled in the lonely darkness of night. Each time he reached for the bottle, he was not just failing himself but also failing Priya, his innocent daughter who deserved a better father.

CHAPTER THIRTEEN

Like Father Like Son!

The air tasted of despair— stale, bitter, thick with the ghosts of empty promises. Sunlight struggled to penetrate the drawn curtains, casting sickly shadows across the debris-strewn floor. Empty bottles clinked softly as Dhruv's bare feet shuffled through the chaos, each step a treacherous dance through a minefield of glass and regret.

Time it had become a meaningless blur, days bleeding into nights and back again without distinction. How long had it been since Priya's death? Weeks? Months? The calendar on the wall remained frozen on the date of her passing, its pages untouched, a silent testament to the moment Dhruv's world had shattered.

He stumbled to the kitchenette, his hand trembling as he reached for the half-empty bottle of whiskey on the counter. The amber liquid sloshed invitingly, promising a few hours of blessed numbness. Dhruv didn't bother with a glass; he lifted the bottle to his lips and took a long, burning swallow.

The familiar warmth spread through his chest, dulling the edges of his grief for a moment. But it wasn't enough. It was never enough. He fumbled in his pocket for his pack of bidis, the thin, hand-rolled cigarettes a comforting weight in his palm. With practised ease, he lit one, inhaling deeply and letting the harsh smoke fill his lungs.

As he exhaled, Dhruv caught a glimpse of his reflection in the grimy window. The face that stared back at him was a stranger's— hollow-cheeked, eyes sunken and bloodshot, a scraggly beard obscuring his once-youthful features. For a moment, superimposed over his reflection, he saw his father's ghost, Ram. The same haunted eyes, the same defeated slump of the shoulders.

The realisation sent a jolt of revulsion through him, and Dhruv stumbled backward, nearly losing his footing on the cluttered floor. He was becoming the very thing he had spent his entire life running from. The bottle slipped from his grasp, shattering on the floor and sending shards of glass skittering across the room.

"Fuck," Dhruv muttered, his voice hoarse from disuse and smoke. He stared at the spreading puddle of whiskey, watching it seep into the cracks. It was a fitting metaphor for his life– spilled and wasted, impossible to reclaim.

The sudden buzz of his phone startled him from his reverie. Dhruv fished it out of his pocket, squinting at the screen. It was a message from Mrs. Roy, his mother-in-law.

"We're bringing Priya over in an hour. Please make sure the place is suitable for a child."

Panic clawed at Dhruv's chest. He looked around the disaster zone of his apartment, knowing there was no way he could make it presentable in such a short time. But the thought of his daughter – his beautiful, innocent little girl – seeing him like this, seeing the squalor he lived in, was unbearable.

With frantic energy, Dhruv began to clean. He gathered bottles and cans, shoving them into garbage bags. He swept up cigarette butts and ashes, sprayed air freshener to mask the lingering odours. But it was a losing battle. The stench of neglect and despair had seeped into every surface, a tangible reminder of his descent.

As he worked, memories of Priya – his wife, not his daughter – flooded his mind. Her radiant smile, the sound of her laughter, the way her eyes crinkled at the corners when she was truly happy. The life they had built together, the dreams they had shared, all turned to ash in the wake of her death.

In the aftermath, Dhruv had been left adrift, a ship without an anchor. The grief had been all-consuming, a black hole that devoured every scrap of joy and hope. He had tried to stay strong for their newborn daughter, but the weight of responsibility coupled with his overwhelming loss had proven too much to bear.

At first, it had been just a drink or two to help him sleep, to quiet the screaming void in his chest. Then, it became a necessity, the only way to make it through the day. The bidis followed soon after, a habit he had kicked years ago resurfacing with a vengeance.

Before he knew it, Dhruv had lost his job at MedTech, the promising career he had built crumbling like a house of cards. His in-laws had stepped in to care for Priya, their concern for their granddaughter outweighing their grief. At the time, Dhruv had been grateful for the help, too lost in his pain to see it for what it was – the beginning of the end.

A sharp knock at the door jolted Dhruv back to the present. He glanced at his phone – barely thirty minutes had passed. His in-laws were early, and he was nowhere near ready.

Taking a deep breath, Dhruv straightened his rumpled shirt and ran a hand through his unkempt hair. He knew it was a futile gesture, but it was all he could do. With trembling fingers, he unlocked the door and pulled it open.

Mr. and Mrs. Roy stood in the hallway, their faces a study in contrast. Mrs. Roy's expression was a weary concern, her eyes searching Dhruv's face for any sign of improvement. Mr. Roy, on the other hand, regarded him with thinly veiled disgust, his lips pressed into a tight line of disapproval.

Between them stood Priya, barely a year old, clutching her grandmother's hand. She looked up at Dhruv with wide, curious eyes – Priya's eyes, he realised with a pang. The same warm brown, flecked with gold, that had captivated him from the moment he first met his wife.

"Dhruv," Mrs. Roy said softly, her voice tinged with pity. "May we come in?"

He stepped aside wordlessly, shame burning in his chest as his in-laws entered the apartment. Despite his best efforts, the place was still a mess. The acrid smell of smoke lingered, mingling with the sickly-sweet scent of spilled alcohol.

Mr. Roy's nose wrinkled in distaste as he surveyed the room. "This is no place for a child," he muttered, loud enough for Dhruv to hear.

Mrs. Roy shot her husband a warning glance before turning back to Dhruv. "We thought it would be good for Priya to spend some time with her father," she said, her tone carefully neutral. "It's been a while since your last visit."

Dhruv nodded, unable to meet her gaze. How long had it been? Weeks? Months? The days blurred together in an alcohol-soaked haze, punctuated only by the occasional, guilt-ridden visits to his in-laws' home.

Priya toddled forward, her chubby hands reaching for a discarded bidi packet on the coffee table. With lightning-fast reflexes born of parental instinct, Mrs. Roy scooped her up before she could touch it.

"Perhaps we should go to the park instead," she suggested, her smile strained. "It's a lovely day outside."

Dhruv nodded mutely, grateful for the suggestion. The thought of his daughter in this squalid apartment made his stomach churn with self-loathing.

Dhruv lagged as they went to the nearby park, watching as his in-laws doted on Priya. They cooed and fussed over her, their faces lighting up with genuine joy at her every gurgle and giggle. It was a stark contrast to the tense, disapproving looks they cast in his direction.

At the park, Mrs. Roy settled Priya into a swing, gently pushing her while Mr. Roy hovered nearby, ready to catch her if needed. Dhruv stood off to the side, feeling like an intruder in this family tableau.

"She's growing so fast," Mrs. Roy commented, her eyes never leaving her granddaughter. "She'll be walking properly any day now."

The words were like a knife to Dhruv's heart. He was missing everything, all the precious milestones of his daughter's life slipping by while he drowned himself in whiskey and smoke.

Mr. Roy's voice cut through his thoughts, sharp and accusatory. "You're not fit to care for her," he said, gesturing back towards the apartment building. "Priya would be ashamed."

The words hung in the air, heavy and undeniable. Dhruv opened his mouth to protest and defend himself, but no words came. What could he say? Mr. Roy was right.

Mrs. Roy placed a hand on her husband's arm, a silent plea for restraint. "We're worried about you, Dhruv," she said softly. "This isn't what Priya would have wanted for you or your daughter."

Dhruv's eyes burned with unshed tears. He knew they were right and that he was failing not just himself but the memory of his wife and his child's future. But the knowledge only deepened his despair, driving him further into the comforting oblivion of addiction.

"I'm trying," he whispered, the lie tasting bitter on his tongue.

Mr. Roy scoffed, turning away to focus on his granddaughter. Mrs. Roy's eyes softened with pity, and somehow, that was worse than her husband's open disdain.

"We're here if you need help," she said, reaching out to squeeze Dhruv's hand. "You're not alone in this."

But he was alone. Utterly, devastatingly alone. The hole left by Priya's death was a gaping wound that no amount of well-meaning concern could fill.

The rest of the visit passed in a blur of forced small talk and tense silence. Dhruv made a few fumbling attempts to interact with his daughter, but she shied away from this stranger who smelled of smoke and sadness. Each time she turned to her grandparents for comfort, Dhruv felt another piece of his heart crumble.

As they prepared to leave, Mr. Roy pulled Dhruv aside. His voice was low, but there was no mistaking the steel beneath his words. "We can't keep doing this," he said. "For Priya's sake, you need to get your act together. If you can't... we'll have to make some difficult decisions."

The threat hung in the air between them, unspoken but clear. Dhruv nodded numbly, watching his in-laws walk away, taking his daughter with them. The sight of Priya's face peering over Mrs. Roy's shoulder, those familiar brown eyes regarding him with innocent curiosity, was almost more than he could bear.

As soon as they were out of sight, Dhruv ran back to his apartment. His hands shook as he fumbled with his keys, desperate to escape the judging eyes of the world and retreat into his self-imposed exile.

Once inside, he made a beeline for the kitchen, yanking open cabinets until he found what he was looking for – a fresh bottle of whiskey hidden behind a stack of dusty plates. He didn't bother with a glass, gulping directly from the bottle, relishing the burn as it slid down his throat.

The bidi was next, and the ritual of lighting it and taking that first deep drag was as familiar and comforting as a lullaby. As the nicotine hit his system, Dhruv felt the tension in his muscles begin to ease, the trembling in his hands subsiding.

He sank onto the worn couch, ash from the bidi falling unheeded onto his shirt. The silence of the apartment pressed in on him, broken only by the occasional distant sound of traffic or a neighbour's muffled voice.

In this quiet moment, with the alcohol warming his blood and the smoke curling around him like a lover's embrace, Dhruv allowed himself to remember.

He thought of Priya, not as she had been in those final, terrible moments, but as she had been when they first met. She had been a force of nature, brilliant and driven, with a laugh that could light up a room.

Dhruv remembered their first date, the carefully chosen Goan restaurant, the scent of jasmine and spices hanging in the air. He could almost taste the coconut water, feel the brush of their fingers as he'd offered her a sip, masking the burn of the chilli she'd playfully complained about.

He remembered their wedding day, Priya radiant in red and gold, her eyes shining joy and promise as they took pheras.

He remembered the day they found out they were expecting, the mix of terror and joy as they imagined their future as parents.

He remembered the joy of holding their daughter for the first time, mixed with the gut-wrenching knowledge that Priya was slipping away.

And then, the memories came faster, sharper. The doctor's words, a hammer blow to his heart: "We may not be able to save them both". He had been forced to make the impossible choice: "Save Priya".

A sob tore from Dhruv's throat, raw and primal. He curled in on himself, the bottle slipping from his grasp and rolling across the floor. The bidi burned forgotten between his fingers, ash accumulating in a neat cylinder.

"I'm sorry," he whispered to the empty room, his wife's ghost, and the daughter he was failing. "I'm so sorry."

But sorry wasn't enough. It wouldn't bring Priya back. It wouldn't erase the disappointment in his in-laws' eyes. It wouldn't give his daughter the father she deserved.

Dhruv's gaze fell on a framed photo on the cluttered coffee table. It was from happier times – he and Priya on their honeymoon, standing on a beach with the sun setting behind them. They looked so young, so full of hope and promise. What had happened to that man? Where had he gone?

With trembling hands, Dhruv picked up the photo. His fingertips traced the outline of Priya's face, smudging the glass with ash and grime. "I don't know how to do this without you," he murmured. "I don't know how to be a father. I don't know how to live."

The silence offered no answers. Outside, the sun was setting, painting the sky in shades of orange and pink. Another day was ending, slipping away into the relentless march of time. Soon, it would be dark, and Dhruv would be left alone with his demons once more.

He reached for the bottle again, needing the numbing embrace of alcohol to quiet the screaming in his head. But as his fingers closed around the cool glass, a memory surfaced – unbidden and unwelcome.

It was from his childhood, one of the rare quiet moments between his father's drunken rages. Ram had been sober for once, sitting at the kitchen table with his head in his hands. Young Dhruv had crept closer, curious about this unfamiliar version of his father.

"Why do you drink, Baba?" he had asked, his child's voice high and clear in the room's stillness.

Ram had looked up, his bloodshot eyes focusing on Dhruv with difficulty. "Because, beta," he had said, his voice rough with emotion and years of hard living, "it makes me forget. But the forgetting... it's a curse, not a blessing."

At the time, Dhruv hadn't understood. Now, as he sat surrounded by the wreckage of his life, the meaning of his father's words hit him with the force of a physical blow.

He was becoming his father. The realisation sent a chill down his spine. Every bottle, every bidi, every day lost to the haze of addiction was a step closer to becoming the man he had sworn he would never be.

Dhruv's hand tightened on the bottle, knuckles white with tension. For a long moment, he sat frozen, caught between the siren call of oblivion and the terrifying prospect of facing his pain sober.

The sound of his phone buzzing broke the spell. Dhruv fumbled for it, nearly dropping it in his haste. It was a message from Mrs. Roy – a photo of Priya, fast asleep in her crib, one tiny hand curled around a stuffed elephant.

The sight of his daughter, peaceful and innocent, unaware of the turmoil in her father's life, was like a punch to the gut. Dhruv stared at the image, taking in every detail of Priya's face. She looked like her mother – the same delicate nose and long eyelashes resting against chubby cheeks.

What would Priya think of him when she was old enough to understand?

CHAPTER FOURTEEN

The Wake-Up Call

The sharp smell of bidi smoke hung heavy in the air, mingling with the sour stench of stale alcohol. Dhruv sat slumped in his worn armchair, his eyes unfocused, staring at nothing. The small apartment, once a sanctuary of love and hope, now felt like a prison of memories and regrets. Empty bottles littered the floor, a testament to his desperate attempts to numb the pain that gnawed at his soul.

The sudden shrill ring of his phone pierced through the haze of his thoughts. Dhruv blinked slowly, his hand fumbling across the cluttered side table until his fingers closed around the vibrating device. He squinted at the screen, the unknown number swimming before his eyes.

"Hello?" His voice was hoarse, barely above a whisper.

"Is this Dhruv?" The voice on the other end was crisp and professional. "This is Dr. Gupta from City Hospital."

Dhruv's heart skipped a beat. The last time he'd received a call from a hospital... No, he couldn't think about that now. "Yes, this is Dhruv," he managed to croak out.

"I'm calling about your father, Ram. He's been admitted to our care, and I'm afraid his condition is critical." The doctor's words seemed to come from far away, muffled by the sudden roaring in Dhruv's ears. "He's asked to see you.

We don't expect him to last more than a few days."

Dhruv's grip on the phone tightened, his knuckles turning white. His father. The man who had haunted his nightmares for years, whose very name could send a shiver of fear down his spine. The man he had sworn never to see again.

"Mr. Dhruv? Are you there?"

He realised he had been silent for too long. "Yes," he said, his voice sounding strange to his ears. "I'm here."

"Your father is asking for you. I understand family situations can be complicated, but seeing you might make his final moments more tolerable. Will you come?"

Would he go? Dhruv's mind reeled, memories flooding in like a torrent. The sting of the belt against his skin, the stink of alcohol on his father's breath, the sound of breaking glass and his mother's muffled sobs. Years of pain and fear condensed into a single moment.

But then, unbidden, another memory surfaced. Priya's gentle touch on his arm, her eyes full of love and understanding. "Your past doesn't define you, Dhruv," she had said. "It's what you choose to do now that matters."

Priya. The thought of her sent a fresh wave of grief crashing over him. She had believed in him, had seen the good in him even when he couldn't see it himself. What would she want him to do?

"Mr. Dhruv?" The doctor's voice pulled him back to the present.

"I'll come," Dhruv heard himself say as if from a great distance. "I'll be there soon."

The journey to the hospital passed in a blur. Dhruv moved as if in a dream, his body on autopilot while his mind churned with memories and emotions. The sterile smell of disinfectant hit him as he entered the hospital, and suddenly, he was transported back in time.

He saw himself, younger and full of hope, rushing through these same doors with Priya. Her face was pale, her hand clutching her swollen belly as contractions wracked her body. The fear that had gripped him then, the desperate prayers he had muttered under his breath. "Please, let them be okay. Please, I'll do anything..."

But his prayers had gone unanswered. Priya had slipped away, leaving Dhruv alone in a world devoid of colour and warmth.

"Mr. Dhruv?" A voice pulled him from his reverie. He saw a middle-aged man in a white coat approaching him. "I'm Dr. Gupta. Thank you for coming."

Dhruv nodded, unable to form words. The doctor's face was kind, but the gravity in his eyes spoke volumes.

"Your father doesn't have much time left," Dr. Gupta said gently. "His liver has finally given out after years of abuse. He's been asking for you. Are you ready to see him?"

Ready? How could anyone be prepared for this? Dhruv wanted to laugh, to cry, to run away. But instead, he found himself nodding again, following the doctor down the hallway.

The room was dim; the only sound was the rhythmic beeping of machines. And there, on the bed, lay a figure that Dhruv barely recognised as his father. Ram's once-imposing frame had withered away, his skin sallow and tightened over his bones. Tubes and wires snaked around him as if trying to tether his fading life to this world.

Dhruv approached the bed slowly, his feet feeling like lead. He sank into the chair beside it, his eyes fixed on the frail form of the man who had loomed so large in his nightmares. How could this be the same person who had terrorised his childhood?

Ram's eyes fluttered open, cloudy and unfocused. They roamed the room before settling on Dhruv's face. A spark of recognition lit them, and his cracked lips moved, forming a word.

"Dhruv," Ram whispered, his voice barely audible through the oxygen mask.

Dhruv leaned closer, a storm of emotions raging within him: anger, fear, pity, and something else he couldn't quite name. "Baba," he said, the word feeling foreign on his tongue after so many years.

Ram's hand, trembling and weak, reached out. Dhruv hesitated momentarily before taking it, marvelling at how small and fragile it felt.

With a herculean effort, Ram gestured towards his oxygen mask. Dhruv understood, gently removing it so his father could speak.

"I…" Ram started, then coughed, a harsh, rattling sound that seemed to shake his entire frame. Dhruv instinctively reached out, then pulled back, his hand hovering awkwardly in the space between them.

"It's alright, Baba," Dhruv mumbled, surprised at the tremor in his voice.

Ram's gaze shifted to their hands, his cloudy eyes seeming to track Dhruv's hesitant movements. "I see… her… sometimes… in you.

The mention of his mother, a phantom presence that had haunted Dhruv's life for so long, sliced through him. It was a low blow, even for a dying man. He started to rise, the familiar anger flaring. "What's the point of this, Baba?" he spat, his voice thick with years of unexpressed rage.

But Ram continued, his voice a faint rasp, as if speaking were a monumental effort. "She… she left because of me." He coughed again, this time a wet, guttural sound that sent a chill down Dhruv's spine.

"I... I destroyed everything." Ram's gaze, unblinking, held Dhruv captive. "I'm sorry," Ram rasped, each word a struggle. "So sorry."

Dhruv felt as if he'd been punched in the gut. Sorry? How could two simple words encompass the years of pain, the shattered childhood, the scars both visible and invisible that Dhruv carried with him every day? How dare he ask for forgiveness when it was too late to change anything?

But as he looked into his father's eyes, Dhruv saw something he had never seen before— regret, deep and genuine. The man before him was not the towering, terrifying figure of his youth but a broken, lonely old man facing the end of his life.

"Baba," Dhruv said again, his voice choked with emotion. He didn't know if he could forgive, didn't know if he wanted to. But at that moment, this wasn't the man who had ruled their lives with anger and violence. This was a broken man grappling with the weight of his past.

For a moment, neither of them spoke. The only sound was the steady beep of the heart monitor, marking the passing seconds of Ram's life. It was then that Dhruv saw it – a single tear tracing a path down his father's cheek.

Ram's hand, impossibly frail, found Dhruv's. His grip was surprisingly firm. "Don't," he whispered, each word laboured. "Don't... be like me.

The words hit Dhruv like a physical blow. In that instant, he saw himself clearly for the first time in months. The bottles strewn around his apartment, the haze of smoke and alcohol that had become his constant companion, the neglect of his daughter— he had become the very thing he had sworn never to be. He had become his father.

Memories of Priya flooded his mind: her smile, her unwavering belief in him, her dreams for their future. "You'll be an amazing father," she had told him, her eyes shining with love and trust. "I know it."

Shame washed over Dhruv. He had failed her and failed their daughter. He had failed himself.

Ram's grip on his hand loosened, his eyes sliding shut. The machines began to beep more urgently. Dr. Gupta rushed in, checking vitals and adjusting equipment. But Dhruv knew, with a certainty that settled in his bones, that these were his father's final moments.

He leaned close, whispering in Ram's ear. "I hear you, Baba. I understand now."

And then, with a final, shuddering breath and a faint smile, Ram Sharma was gone.

The continuous tone of the heart monitor filled the room, a final punctuation to a life filled with regret and missed opportunities.

Dhruv sat there for a long time, still holding his father's hand as it grew cold. He was vaguely aware of Dr. Gupta entering the room, nurses bustling around, and forms being pressed into his hands to sign. But it all felt distant, unreal. The anger and fear that had defined their relationship for so long seemed to have drained away, leaving behind a hollow sadness and a glimmer of something that might, one day, become understanding.

It wasn't until he stepped out of the hospital into the cool night air that the reality of what had happened began to sink in. His father was gone. The man who had been the source of so much pain in his life, but also the man whose blood ran through his veins, whose features he saw every time he looked in the mirror.

Dhruv lit a bidi with trembling hands, inhaling deeply. The familiar burn in his lungs was comforting, grounding. But for the first time in months, it didn't bring the numbness he craved. Instead, he felt... everything. The grief for his father tangled up with years of anger and fear. The ache of losing Priya, still raw and bleeding. The shame of abandoning his daughter.

He started walking, with no particular destination in mind. The streets were quiet at this late hour, with the occasional car passing by and the distant sound of a dog barking. Dhruv walked and smoked, his mind a whirlwind of memories and emotions.

He thought about his father, about the abuse and the terror of his childhood. But he also thought about the man he had seen in that hospital bed – frail, vulnerable, seeking forgiveness. He thought about the cycle of addiction and violence that had shaped both their lives.

And then, unbidden, he thought about his daughter. The tiny, perfect being he had held in his arms for those brief, precious moments before his world fell apart. He wondered what she looked like now, how much she had grown. He wondered if she ever asked about him.

As the first hints of dawn began to lighten the sky, Dhruv found himself in a small park. He sat heavily on a bench, his body aching from the long night of walking, his mind exhausted from the tumult of emotions.

He lit another bidi, his last one, and stared at it for a long moment. Then, with a sudden, decisive movement, he crushed it out, unopened, on the bench beside him.

Dhruv took a deep breath, feeling the cool morning air fill his lungs. For the first time in months, his head felt clear. The colours were sharper, the air clearer. The grief was still there, the pain still raw. But alongside it was something else.

The weight of his father's last words, the memory of Priya's faith in him, the thought of his daughter growing up without her parents— it all pressed down on him, threatening to crush him.

He couldn't change the past. He couldn't undo the years of abuse he had suffered, or bring Priya back, or erase the months he had lost to grief and addiction. But he could change the future. He could break the cycle that had trapped both him and his father.

As the sun began to rise, painting the sky in shades of pink and gold, Dhruv made a decision. He would get help. He would face his addiction, his grief, and his trauma. And then, when he was stronger, he would find his daughter. He would be the father she deserved, the father he had never had.

It wouldn't be easy. The road ahead was long and fraught with challenges. But as Dhruv sat there, watching the new day dawn, he felt something he hadn't felt in a very long time.

Hope.

The wake-up call had come in the form of his father's death. But the choice to answer it, to change, to heal— that was all Dhruv's. And for the first time in months, he felt ready to make that choice.

Dhruv stood up as the city around him began to stir to life. He took one last look at the crushed bidi on the bench, a symbol of the life he was leaving behind.

Then, with a deep breath and squared shoulders, he began to walk.

Towards help. Towards healing. Towards hope.

Towards a future, he could barely imagine but was finally ready to fight for.

With trembling fingers, he pulled out his phone and dialled a number he hadn't used in far too long.

"Di?" he said when the call connected. "It's Dhruv. I... I need help."

As he spoke those words, Dhruv felt something shift inside him. It wasn't hope, not yet. But it was a start. A chance to honour Priya's memory, to be the father his daughter deserved, to become the man he had always wanted to be.

The road ahead would be long and difficult. There would be struggles and setbacks, moments of doubt and despair. But as Dhruv ended the call with Sunita, setting the first steps of his recovery in motion, he felt a flicker of something he hadn't experienced in a long time.

It felt like a possibility. It felt like the dawn after a long night. It felt, ever so faintly, like the beginnings of redemption.

CHAPTER FIFTEEN

The Long Road Back

Dhruv's world had become a haze of nausea and tremors. The stark white walls of the rehab centre seemed to pulse and waver as if they, too, were caught in the throes of withdrawal. He lay on his bed, sheets damp with sweat, his body a battleground of conflicting sensations. The absence of alcohol and nicotine left a void that his body desperately sought to fill, screaming its discontent through every nerve ending.

Detox was hell.

The first week was a blur of sleepless nights and restless days. Dhruv's hands shook uncontrollably, making even holding a glass of water a Herculean task. His skin crawled with a constant, maddening itch that no amount of scratching could satisfy. It felt as if an army of insects had taken up residence just beneath the surface, marching relentlessly across his flesh.

Nausea was a constant companion, rising in waves that left him hunched over the toilet, heaving until there was nothing left but bitter bile. The taste in his mouth was foul, a lingering reminder of the poison he had willingly poured into his body for months. Even water tasted wrong, as if his taste buds had forgotten how to process anything that wasn't laced with alcohol.

Sleep, when it came, was fitful and plagued by nightmares. Dhruv would jolt awake, drenched in sweat, his heart pounding as if trying to escape his chest. In those moments between sleeping and waking, reality blurred. He would see Priya, her face pale and accusing, or his father looming over him with a belt in hand. The ghosts of his past and present merged into a terrifying tapestry that left him gasping for air.

Dr. Mukherjee, the chief psychiatrist at the centre, had warned him about the hallucinations. "Your brain is recalibrating," she had explained in her calm, steady voice. "It's trying to make sense of a world without the chemicals it had grown accustomed to. What you're experiencing is normal, Dhruv. Difficult, yes, but normal."

` Normal. The word seemed absurd in the face of what he was going through. How could this hell be considered normal? Yet, as the days crawled by, Dhruv began to notice small improvements. The shaking in his hands lessened incrementally. The nausea, while still present, became more manageable. Sleep, though still disturbed, came a little easier each night.

It was during his second week that Dhruv first attended a group therapy session. He had resisted initially, the thought of sharing his pain with strangers seeming impossible. But Dr. Mukherjee had been gently insistent, and so he found himself sitting in a circle of plastic chairs, surrounded by faces that bore the same haunted look he saw in the mirror each morning.

The room smelled of disinfectant and stale coffee, an oddly comforting combination that spoke of healing and shared struggles. Dhruv's palms were sweaty as he gripped the edges of his chair, his eyes darting from face to face, searching for judgment and finding only understanding.

A middle-aged woman with tired eyes and a kind smile introduced herself as the group facilitator. "We're here to share our stories," she said, her voice warm and encouraging. "To understand that we're not alone in our struggles. Who would like to start?"

Silence stretched out, heavy and expectant. Dhruv's heart raced, his breath coming in short, sharp gasps. He wanted to speak, to let out the torrent of pain and guilt that had been building inside him for months, years even. But the words stuck in his throat, trapped behind a lifetime of learned silence.

It was a young man, barely out of his teens, who finally broke the silence. "I'm Ajay," he said, his voice cracking slightly. "And I... I don't know how to live without being high anymore."

As Ajay spoke, Dhruv felt something shift inside him. The young man's words, raw and honest, struck a chord. He saw in Ajay's trembling hands and haunted eyes a reflection of his own pain. And as others in the group began to share their stories— tales of loss, of trauma, of desperate attempts to numb the pain— Dhruv felt the walls he had built around himself begin to crumble.

When it came to his turn, Dhruv took a deep breath. His voice, when it came, was barely above a whisper. "My name is Dhruv," he said, the words feeling foreign on his tongue. "And I... I'm here because I'm afraid of becoming my father."

The admission hung in the air, heavy with implication. Dhruv felt exposed, vulnerable in a way he had never allowed himself to be before. But as he looked around the circle, he saw only nods of understanding, eyes that reflected back his own pain and fear.

"Can you tell us more about that, Dhruv?" the facilitator gently prompted.

Dhruv closed his eyes, memories washing over him in a flood. The sting of his father's belt, the acrid smell of cheap whiskey on his breath, the sound of his mother's muffled sobs. He opened his mouth, and the words began to pour out.

"My father... he was an alcoholic. Violent. Every night was a gamble— would he pass out before or after using his fists? I swore I'd never be like him. But now..." Dhruv's voice broke, tears welling up in his eyes. "Now, every time I look in the mirror, every time I fail... I see him. I become him."

The admission felt like ripping off a bandage, exposing a wound that had never truly healed. Dhruv's body shook with silent sobs, years of pent-up emotion finally finding release. He felt a hand on his shoulder, solid and comforting. When he looked up, he saw the facilitator standing beside him, her eyes filled with compassion.

"Dhruv," she said softly, "recognizing that fear is a huge step. But I want you to consider something – your father never sought help. He never tried to break the cycle. You're here. You're trying. That already makes you different."

Those words pierced through the fog of self-loathing that had enveloped Dhruv for so long. He looked around the room, seeing nods of agreement, hearing murmurs of support. For the first time in months, perhaps years, he felt a glimmer of hope.

As the session continued, Dhruv found himself listening with newfound intensity to the stories of others. He recognised pieces of himself in their struggles— the desperate need to escape reality, the guilt, the fear of failing loved ones. But he also saw strength in their determination to change, to break free from the cycles that had trapped them.

When the session ended, Dhruv felt drained but oddly lighter. The weight he had been carrying for so long hadn't disappeared, but it felt more manageable.

As he made his way back to his room, Dhruv's mind was a whirlwind of thoughts and emotions. The raw honesty of the group session had shaken something loose inside him. He felt exposed, vulnerable, but also strangely empowered. For the first time, he had given voice to his deepest fears, and the world hadn't ended. Instead, he had found understanding and support.

That night, as Dhruv lay in his bed, the familiar cravings gnawing at him, he found himself thinking not of the bottle that had been his solace for so long, but of the faces in that group. Of Ajay, barely more than a boy, fighting battles no one his age should have to face. Of the middle-aged woman with kind eyes who had shared her story of losing everything to addiction before finally seeking help.

And he thought of Priya. Sweet, vibrant Priya, who had seen the best in him even when he couldn't see it himself. Who had believed in his strength even as he doubted it. The pain of her loss was still a raw wound, but for the first time, Dhruv allowed himself to think of her without immediately reaching for the numbing embrace of alcohol.

Instead, he closed his eyes and pictured her smile, how her eyes crinkled at the corners when she laughed. He remembered the warmth of her hand in his, the soft curve of her pregnant belly in those final, precious months. And as sleep finally claimed him, Dhruv's dreams were not of nightmares and loss but of hope and the possibility of redemption.

The next few weeks passed in a blur of therapy sessions, both group and individual and the slow, painful process of relearning how to live without the crutch of addiction. Dr. Mukherjee became a constant presence in Dhruv's life, and her calm demeanour and insightful questions helped him navigate the treacherous waters of his psyche.

"Addiction," she explained during one of their sessions, "is often a symptom of deeper issues. It's a maladaptive coping mechanism. Our job is to identify those underlying issues and develop healthier ways to address them."

Dhruv nodded, his fingers absently tracing the scars on his arms— faded reminders of his father's cruelty. "I thought I had dealt with all that," he admitted. "I got out, made something of myself. I thought I had left it all behind."

Dr. Mukherjee leaned forward, her eyes kind but intense. "Trauma doesn't just disappear, Dhruv. It shapes us. It influences our behaviours in ways we might not even recognise. But recognising its impact is the first step towards true healing."

As the days passed, Dhruv found himself opening up more, not just in therapy but in his interactions with other patients. He formed a particularly close bond with Ajay, the young man from his first group session. They often sat together during meals, sharing stories of their pasts and hopes for the future.

"I want to go back to school," Ajay confided one day, pushing his food around his plate. "Maybe become a counsellor or something. Help kids like us, you know?"

Dhruv felt a surge of affection for the younger man. "That's a great goal," he said, meaning it. "You'd be good at it, I think. You've got a way of making people feel heard."

Ajay's face lit up at the compliment, and Dhruv was struck by how young he looked. It was a stark reminder of how addiction could rob people of their youth and their potential. But it also highlighted the resilience of the human spirit and the capacity for hope even in the darkest times.

As Dhruv progressed in his recovery, he found the courage to reach out to his in-laws, the Roys. The first few conversations were awkward, stilted affairs, full of long pauses and unspoken recriminations. But underlying it all was a shared love for little Priya, a common ground that allowed them to push past their initial discomfort.

It was Mrs. Roy who made the first genuine overture. She arrived at the rehab centre one sunny afternoon, a small photo album tucked under her arm. Dhruv met her in the visitor's area, his heart pounding with anticipation and dread.

Mrs. Roy looked older than he remembered, lines of grief etched deeply into her face. But there was a softness in her eyes as she looked at him, a hint of the warmth that had always made him feel welcome in their home.

"Dhruv," she said, her voice barely above a whisper. "You're looking better."

Dhruv nodded, not trusting himself to speak. Mrs. Roy sat across from him, placing the album on the table between them.

"Priya made this," she said softly, pushing it towards him. "She was going to give it to you after the baby was born. I think... I think she'd want you to have it now."

Dhruv's hands shook as he reached for the album. The cover was a soft blue, decorated with delicate silver stars—so quintessentially Priya that it made his heart ache. He opened it slowly, almost reverently.

Inside were photos of him and Priya, moments big and small captured throughout their relationship. There they were on their first date, both looking nervous and excited. In a candid shot from a friend's wedding, Dhruv looking at Priya with undisguised adoration as she laughed at something off-camera. Their wedding day, surrounded by friends and family, their faces alight with joy.

As Dhruv turned the pages, he felt tears welling in his eyes. Each photo was a reminder of the life they had built together and the love they had shared. It was beautiful and painful, a bittersweet testament to what he had lost.

On the last page, a sonogram picture was carefully placed. Beneath it, in Priya's neat handwriting, were the words: "The best of both of us."

Dhruv traced the words with his finger, tears falling freely now. He looked up at Mrs. Roy, seeing his grief mirrored in her eyes.

"We miss her too," she said, gently squeezing his hand. "And we… we'd like you to be part of our lives. Ours and little Priya's. If you want to."

It was a tentative olive branch, but one Dhruv grasped with both hands. "I'd like that," he managed to say through tears. "I'd like that very much."

That visit marked a turning point in Dhruv's recovery. The knowledge that he wasn't alone. That there were people who cared about him and believed in him gave him renewed strength to face the challenges ahead.

As the weeks turned into months, Dhruv threw himself into his recovery with a determination that surprised even himself. He attended every therapy session, both group and individual, with an openness and honesty that would have been unthinkable a short time ago.

In group therapy, he became a source of support for newer patients, sharing his experiences and offering encouragement. It was a role that felt strange at first, but one that he grew into, finding strength in helping others navigate the same treacherous waters he was still learning to sail.

Dr. Mukherjee noticed the change in him. "You're making remarkable progress, Dhruv," she said during one of their sessions. "But I want you to remember that recovery is not linear. There will be setbacks and moments of doubt. The important thing is to keep moving forward, one day at a time."

Dhruv nodded, taking her words to heart. He had learned the hard way that there were no quick fixes, no magic solutions. Recovery was a daily choice, a constant battle against the demons that had driven him to addiction in the first place.

Dr. Mukherjee encouraged Dhruv to keep a journal as part of his therapy. At first, he felt awkward, unsure of what to write. But as the days passed, he poured his thoughts and feelings onto the pages, using them to process his emotions and track his progress.

He wrote letters to Priya, telling her about their daughter's growth, his progress, his fears and hopes for the future. It was a way of keeping her memory alive, of including her in his journey even if she couldn't be there physically.

Dear Priya,

Little Priya took her first steps today. Your parents sent me a video. She's so determined, just like you were. I wish you could have seen it. I wish you were here to share these moments.

I'm doing better. The cravings are still there but not as overwhelming as they used to be. I'm learning to sit with the discomfort, to face my emotions instead of trying to numb them.

I think about you every day. About the life we had and the future we planned. It still hurts, but I'm trying to honour your memory by being the man you always believed I could be.

I miss you. I love you. Always.

Dhruv

These letters became a lifeline for Dhruv, a way of processing his grief and guilt while also celebrating the small victories in his recovery. They were a reminder of why he was fighting so hard to stay sober— for himself, for his daughter, and for the memory of the woman who had loved him at his best and his worst.

As Dhruv's time in rehab drew to a close, he found himself facing a new set of challenges. The prospect of returning to the outside world was daunting with all its temptations and triggers. But he was no longer the broken man who had entered the facility months ago.

As Dhruv's time in rehab drew to a close, he found himself facing a new set of challenges. The prospect of returning to the outside world was daunting with all its temptations and triggers. But he was no longer the broken man who had entered the facility months ago.

In his final session with Dr. Mukherjee, Dhruv voiced his fears. "What if I can't do this? What if I slip up?"

Dr. Mukherjee leaned forward. Her eyes met his with unwavering confidence. "Dhruv, recovery isn't about never stumbling. It's about learning to pick yourself up when you do. You've built a strong foundation here, but the real work begins when you leave."

She handed him a small card with a list of local support group meetings and her office number. "Remember, you're not alone in this journey. Reach out when you need help. It's not a sign of weakness but of strength."

Dhruv nodded, clutching the card like a lifeline. As he packed his meagre belongings, a mix of anticipation and anxiety swirled in his gut. The rehab centre had become a safe haven with its structured routines and constant support. The world outside seemed vast and fraught with potential pitfalls.

The day of his release dawned bright and clear, a stark contrast to the tumultuous emotions roiling within him. As Dhruv stood at the entrance of the rehab centre, his duffel bag at his feet, he took a deep breath, filling his lungs with the crisp morning air. It tasted of possibility and second chances.

To his surprise, he found Mr. and Mrs. Roy waiting for him. Mrs. Roy stepped forward, enveloping him in a warm embrace. "Welcome back, beta," she whispered, her voice thick with emotion. Mr. Roy, ever the more reserved of the two, offered a firm handshake and a nod of approval.

"We thought you might like a ride home," Mr. Roy said, gesturing to their car. "And perhaps... perhaps you'd like to see Priya?"

Dhruv felt his heart skip a beat. He had seen photos and videos of his daughter over the past months, but the prospect of seeing her in person, of holding her, was overwhelming. He nodded, not trusting his voice to remain steady.

The drive to the Roys' home was filled with a comfortable silence, punctuated by Mrs. Roy's occasional updates about Priya's latest achievements. Dhruv listened intently, drinking in every detail, trying to bridge the gap of the months he had missed.

As they pulled into the driveway of the familiar house, Dhruv felt a lump form in his throat. This was once his home, where he and Priya had dreamed of raising their family. Now, he felt like a stranger, an intruder in a life that no longer belonged to him.

Mrs. Roy seemed to sense his hesitation. She placed a gentle hand on his arm. "She's been asking for you, you know. In her way. We've shown her your picture every day.

Summoning his courage, Dhruv followed the Roys into the house. The sound of babbling and soft laughter drifted from the living room. As they rounded the corner, Dhruv's breath caught in his throat.

There, sitting on a colourful play mat, was his daughter. Priya had grown so much in the months he'd been away. Her dark curls framed a face that was the spitting image of her mother, but her eyes— those were unmistakably his.

For a moment, the world seemed to stand still. Then, Priya looked up, her eyes widening with recognition. "Da!" she exclaimed, her chubby arms reaching out towards him.

Dhruv fell to his knees beside her, gathering her into his arms. Her feel, solid and real, broke something open inside him. Tears flowed freely as he held his daughter close, breathing in her sweet baby scent.

"I'm here, beta," he whispered, his voice choked with emotion. "Papa's here. I'm so sorry I was gone for so long."

As he held his daughter, Dhruv felt a shift within himself. The overwhelming love he felt for this tiny being crystallized his resolve. He would stay sober, not just for himself, but for her. She deserved a father she could depend on, one who would be present for all the big and small moments ahead.

The next few weeks were a whirlwind of adjustments and new routines. Dhruv moved into a small apartment near the Roys', close enough to be a daily presence in Priya's life, but he maintained his independence to focus on his recovery.

Returning to work presented its own set of challenges. Dhruv had been honest with his superiors at MedTech about his struggles and his time in rehab. To his relief, they had been surprisingly understanding. They worked out a flexible schedule that allowed him to balance his job with his recovery and responsibilities as a single father.

His first day back at the office was a study of mixed emotions. There were curious glances and whispered conversations that fell silent as he walked by. But some colleagues welcomed him back warmly, their genuine concern touching him deeply.

As Dhruv settled back into his work routine, he found that his experiences had given him a new perspective. Problems that would have once sent him spiralling now seemed manageable. He approached challenges with a calm determination, drawing on the coping mechanisms he had learned in rehab.

But it wasn't all smooth sailing. There were days when the cravings hit hard when the weight of his responsibilities felt overwhelming. On one tough afternoon, Dhruv found himself standing outside a liquor store, his hand on the door handle, every fibre of his being screaming for the temporary relief he knew he'd find inside.

In that moment of weakness, he remembered Dr. Mukherjee's words. With trembling hands, he pulled out his phone and dialled Sunita's number.

"I'm outside Malhotra's Wines and Spirits," Dhruv said, his voice shaking. "I... I don't think I can do this, Di."

"Stay right there," Sunita replied without hesitation. "I'm on my way. Just keep talking to me, okay?"

For the next twenty minutes, Dhruv paced outside the store, clutching his phone like a lifeline as Sunita talked him through breathing exercises and reminded him of how far he'd come. By the time Sunita arrived, the worst of the craving had passed, leaving Dhruv drained but grateful.

"You did good calling me," Sunita said as they walked to a nearby park. "That's what we're here for. No one does this alone."

Dhruv felt emotion wash over him as they sat on a bench, watching children play on the swings. "I almost threw it all away," he said, his voice barely above a whisper. "My daughter, my job, everything I've worked for."

Sunita nodded, his eyes understanding. "But you didn't. That's what matters. Recovery isn't about never feeling tempted. It's about what you do when temptation hits."

That evening, as Dhruv tucked Priya into bed, he felt a renewed sense of purpose. He kissed her forehead gently, marvelling at the perfect curve of her cheek, the soft flutter of her eyelashes.

"I promise you, beta," he whispered, "I'll always be here for you. No matter how hard it gets, I'll keep fighting. For both of us."

As the weeks turned into months, Dhruv found himself settling into a new rhythm of life. His days were filled with work, therapy sessions, support group meetings, and precious time with his daughter. It wasn't always easy, but it was real and his.

He continued to write in his journal, documenting his struggles, triumphs, fears, and hopes. Sometimes, when the house was quiet, and Priya was asleep late at night, he would read over his old entries, marvelling at how far he had come.

Dear Priya,

Another milestone today. Six months sober. There are moments when I can hardly believe it myself. The road hasn't been easy, but I wake up clear-headed every day. I am grateful for every moment I spend with our daughter.

I wish you could see her, love. She's growing so fast, changing every day. She has your smile, you know. That same brightness could light up a room. When she laughs, I hear echoes of you.

I'm trying to be the father she deserves, the man you always believed I could be. Some days are harder than others, but I'm learning to take it one day at a time. Your parents have been incredible. I don't know if I could have done this without their support.

I miss you—every day. But I'm learning to carry your memory with me in a way that gives me strength rather than pulling me under. You'll always be a part of us.

All my love,

Dhruv

As Dhruv closed his journal, he heard a soft whimper from the baby monitor. He tiptoed to Priya's room, finding her stirring in her crib. As he lifted her into his arms, her tiny body warm and trusting against his chest, he felt a surge of love so powerful it nearly took his breath away.

At that moment, holding his daughter in the quiet of the night, Dhruv realised something profound. The road to recovery wasn't just about abstaining from alcohol or overcoming his past. It was about being fully and completely present for moments like these. It was about building a future, one day at a time, filled with love, hope, and possibility.

As he gently rocked Priya back to sleep, Dhruv made a silent promise to himself, his daughter, and Priya's memory. He would continue to walk this path of recovery, no matter how difficult it might become. Because now he understood – it wasn't just about surviving. It was about truly learning to live again.

The soft glow of dawn began to paint the sky when Dhruv finally laid Priya back in her crib. He stood there for a moment, watching the gentle rise and fall of her chest, marvelling at the perfect little person he and Priya had created.

As he made his way back to his room, Dhruv paused by the window, looking out at the world slowly coming to life. The city was waking up, street lights flickering off as the sun's first rays touched the horizon. It was a new day full of challenges, opportunities, struggles, and joys.

And he was ready to face it, one moment at a time.

CHAPTER SIXTEEN

Rebuilding

As Priya's first birthday approached, Dhruv felt mixed emotions he couldn't entirely untangle. Joy at his daughter's growth and health, sorrow that Priya wasn't there to see it, pride in his progress, and a deep, abiding gratitude for the support system that had helped him back from the brink.

The day of the birthday party dawned bright and clear. The Roys arrived early to help set up. Their relationship with Dhruv was now warmer, built on a shared love for Priya and a mutual understanding of loss. Sunita came, too, and her presence was a reminder of how far Dhruv had come.

As Dhruv watched Priya smash her hands into her birthday cake, her face lit up with delight. He felt a warmth in his chest that had been absent for too long. It wasn't happiness, not entirely – the absence of Priya was still a constant ache – but it was something close to peace.

That night, after the guests had left and Priya was asleep, Dhruv sat down to write his letter to Priya.

"My love," he began, the words flowing easily after months of practice. "Today was challenging but beautiful, too. Our little girl is growing so fast. She has your spirit, your joy. I wish you could see her.

"I'm doing better. Some days are still a struggle, but I'm fighting. For her, for you, for the man you always believed I could be. I miss you every day, Priya. I think I always will. But I'm learning to carry that love with me without letting it drag me under.

"Little Priya asked about you today. Well, not in words, but she pointed at your picture and made that questioning sound she does. I told her about you, about how much you loved her, how excited you were to meet her. I'll keep telling her every day, so she knows how amazing her mother was.

"I don't know what the future holds, but I promise you this: I'll live like you asked me to. I'll give our daughter the life we dreamed of for her. And I'll keep loving you, always.

"Until tomorrow, my heart.

All my love, Dhruv."

He set down the pen, wiping away the tears falling onto the page. Then, with a deep breath, he stood and walked to the window. The night sky was clear, stars twinkling brightly. Dhruv looked up at them, imagining Priya looking back down at him.

"Goodnight, my love," he whispered to the stars. "Watch over us."

As he returned to the room, his eyes fell on a framed photo of Priya, her radiant smile and full of life. For the first time in a long while, Dhruv smiled back. The road ahead was still long and uncertain, but he was no longer walking alone. He had his daughter, his family, his friends, and the enduring love of the woman who had saved him in more ways than one.

With that thought warming his heart, Dhruv headed to bed, ready to face whatever tomorrow might bring. The grief was still there, a constant companion, but it no longer defined him. He was a father, a survivor, a man learning to live again.

And somewhere, he knew, Priya was proud.

Glossary

Arrey: An exclamation used to express surprise or address someone, similar to "hey" or "oh" in English.

Azulejo: A type of painted, tin-glazed ceramic tile work particularly prominent in Portugal.

Baba: A term of endearment for "father" in many Indian languages.

Bebinca: A traditional Goan dessert, a layered cake made with coconut milk, eggs, sugar, and ghee.

Beta: A term of endearment meaning "son" or "child" in Hindi and other Indian languages.

Bidi: A thin, hand-rolled cigarette with tobacco flakes wrapped in a tendu leaf and tied with a string.

Chai: A spiced tea beverage popular in South Asia, typically made with black tea, milk, sugar, and spices like cardamom, ginger, and cloves.

Daal: A lentil-based stew or soup, a staple in South Asian cuisine.

Di: A term of respect and affection for an older sister or a woman seen as an older sister figure in many Indian languages.

Fado: A genre of Portuguese music typically characterised by mournful tunes and lyrics, often about the sea, fate, or lost love.

Paan: A popular South Asian treat consisting of betel leaf filled with spices, nuts, and sometimes tobacco.

Pheras: The central ritual in a Hindu wedding ceremony, where the bride and groom circle a sacred fire, taking vows.

Roti: A round, flatbread staple in South Asian cuisine.

GLOSSARY

Sabji: A generic term for vegetable dishes in Indian cuisine.

Xacuti: A Goan curry dish, typically made with chicken or lamb, coconut, and a blend of spices.